DUPLICITY, CARE TO DIE?

DUPLICITY, CARE TO DIE?

An Inspector Willis murder mystery by

Ray Klausen

ISBN: 978-1-961869-13-4

Cover design by C. David Pina

Interior design: Thomas Edward West of Amarna Books & Media.

First print edition 2024

Amarna Books & Media
Philadelphia, PA
www.amarnabooksandmedia.net

Dedication

To Jim and Chris Klausen,
My brother and nephew,
Both special in my heart

Acknowledgements

I wish to acknowledge the following people for their help, support, and inspiration in making this book a reality:

David Meitty

Sharon Miller

Ricky Newkirk

H.R. Nicholson

David Pina

Rebecca Sawyer Fae

Thomas Edward West

Table of Contents

Wednesday—Day One: And so it started 1

Thursday—Day Two: The Meeting 8

Friday—Day Three: Laura and some of her friends 35

Saturday—Day Four: There's a killer out there............................. 58

Sunday—Day Five: A disturbing thought begins to grow 116

Monday—Day Six: A distressing aftermath................................. 134

Tuesday—Day Seven: The heart of the matter............................ 155

Wednesday—Day Eight: Rest in Peace... 169

Duplicity:

Deceitfulness or double-meaning

Wednesday—Day One
And so it started

Rosaline O'Connor was watering her plants, even though the TV weatherman had warned that a heavy rainstorm was imminent. Rosaline always watered the plants around her villa come hell or high water, as it was the main activity that gave her public access to the comings and goings of everyone in the immediate neighborhood. She had her pulse on the lifeblood of the enclave nicknamed "The Cove"—short for Willow Cove, one of the higher-end colonies that encircled a small pond in Sunningdale, an exclusive retirement community, in southern Florida.

Rosaline, who was mostly called Roz, was one of those women whose life had somehow shaped her appearance. She had a rather sharp-shaped look about her, very angular with piercing, darting black eyes. She was noted around the community as the unofficial person who tracked the comings and goings of every resident. Her *modus operandi* was based on the proposition that, as the day is long, her neighbors were always up to no good for sure. She was in her early 70s and was, in her mind, the self-proclaimed guardian of her colony, whether her fellow residents liked it or not. Most did not.

She was peering over the hedge at the back of her lawn when her phone rang inside her villa. Having rushed to peek outside earlier to investigate what she perceived as a car crash of some sort—which proved to be a false alarm—she had left her cellphone phone on her dresser near an open window, so, luckily, she heard it.

She quickly hurried in to catch it before she missed the call. Who knows, it might be some valuable gossip, so she rushed to catch the caller before the phone began recording the incoming message. As she rounded the corner of her living room, she felt a sharp pain in her side. She was astounded to look down to see a knife sticking in her side just before losing consciousness and collapsing on the floor.

A figure dressed all in black, including black gloves,

studied Roz's fallen body, carefully took Roz's hand, and pressed it around the handle of the knife. The figure then removed one of Roz's shoes and flipped over an area rug so that it looked like she had tripped on the rug and had accidentally fallen on the knife she was carrying.

Satisfied that it appeared that Rosaline had experienced one of those freak accidents that older people sometimes fall victim to, the figure went to the kitchen, took out an orange from the fridge, placed it on a cutting board and cut it in half. The person then carefully cleaned the knife and replaced it in the wooden knife holder with the rest of the knives, and, satisfied that it looked like Roz had been working in the kitchen and had rushed to answer her phone, tripped, and accidentally fatally stabbed herself. The intruder then quietly slipped out the back door and left Roz to bleed to death as a large pool of blood started to surround her body.

The news of Roz's freak accident sent chills through the surrounding community, with several residents quickly ordering medical alert buttons in the hopes that should the wearer have an accident such as Roz's, he or she might be able to get help in time.

In time, though, life went on and everyone soon forgot Roz's freak accident… that is, everyone but Laura.

It was one of those fine, warm spring days when the weather was so perfect that one felt so glad to be alive. This was especially true for the people at Sunningdale, a fine continuing care facility for the aging and wealthy. Laura Wilk had been living there for about three years and had felt that she had adjusted just fine, despite the constant reminders of the aging process when someone walked by you utilizing a stroller or cane. Initially, Laura was concerned that she might become depressed being surrounded by those reminders of what time can do to a person, but she soon discovered that many of the people at Sunningdale, because of the considerable cost to stay there, tended to be highly successful financially in life and were mostly very interesting and engaging.

They, for the most part, stayed very active. There were constant events such as lectures in the resident theatre, classes to attend, as well as an extensive array of theatre events including plays, opera, and ballet performances available, as Sarasota was extremely supportive of the arts.

The one depressing thought was that one might live too long and run out of money. Luckily, that was the rare exception. There was, of course, the concern that one might suffer a condition that would take over one's life, be it a permanent mobility condition or, worse yet, a cognitive impediment that might unfold during this last stage of one's life. Laura was painfully aware of this, having lost her much older husband two years earlier to a devastating and quick case of progressive dementia. While Laura, being in her late 50s, was a bit young for a Sunningdale occupant, she wasn't the only one who lived in Sunningdale who was youthful in comparison to the majority of the occupants.

That thought aside, today was a glorious spring day with a promise of new life visible in the surrounding colorful flower beds and trees, alive with their vivid crowns of new leaves and flowers. While it appeared to be a time of rebirth and new life, Laura was not in tune with this at all. Normally a very positive and caring person, she had been disturbed by a growing feeling of intense apprehension. And so, she took pen to paper and wrote a letter to Inspector Willis. Normally, she might tackle her computer and try to email her message to Willis, but her concern now seemed so personal that the idea of an internet missive seemed inappropriate... cold.

She also had a secret apprehension that her fears might be discovered and that she might then be in real danger. Being practical and of a certain generation, she felt that a more personal, handwritten letter might prove more effective... more productive. She had always had handsome penmanship and being of clear mind, she picked up her favorite special pen and simply stated her concern to Willis:

My dear Willis,

I'm writing to you because I don't trust the security of sending emails to you. A strange feeling for sure, but strange things have been happening around here in Sunningdale and I'm not sure the internet is secure.

I realize it has been ages since we've talked. As you know, our major connection was your mother Rose, my dear, dear friend. Her passing was and continues to be extremely painful to me. The mere mentioning of Rose's name fills me with such sadness that I've shied away from any reminders of my loss. That loss is, I'm sure, equally as painful for you. Unfortunately, I now have to ask a great favor from you. I've been deeply upset about the recent unexpected passing of several neighbors here in Sunningdale.

As you know, Sunningdale is a continuing care facility where one is supposed to find peace, quiet, and care in one's later years. That doesn't seem to be the current case here. Your mother would have been greatly disturbed over what appears to be happening in this facility. Call me paranoid, but I'm greatly alarmed. I don't want to put what's bothering me in writing but if you can find time in your busy schedule, I would so appreciate it if *you would come here as my guest as soon as possible. I'm desperately distressed, alarmed, and confused. Please come as soon as you're able. I will, of course, cover your expenses.*

With much affection,

Laura

(My phone number is 285 373 9956 should you need to call me)

Willis read the letter with growing concern. It was not like Laura to overreact, so he immediately consulted his schedule and determined that his current project was in its final phase and could easily be handled by either Ross or Monty, his trusted assistants.

He took a deep breath, attacked his computer, and soon had a reservation to fly to Sarasota on Delta Airlines. He then followed this with a brief call to Laura, letting her know that he would be arriving about 2:30 PM the following day.

He next called his assistants, Ross and Monty, and outlined what needed to be done to finalize his latest case, sent off a number of emails to cancel some appointments, and started to pack. Fortunately, his schedule had been fairly light, as he usually was very busy. In any case, this was special. His mother had been great friends with Laura and he felt he owed it to Laura to hear of her problems in person.

Thursday—Day Two
The meeting

The next morning, Willis showered, shaved, packed a bag with enough items to last a week, and grabbed a quick bite of breakfast... a grapefruit scooped out with a special grapefruit spoon he kept handy plus a toasted English muffin and, of course, his two cups of coffee, black, no cream, no sugar. He double-checked his cell phone for messages, quickly answered the important ones, and took an Uber to the airport. Normally, he would have driven there and put his car in the long-term parking lot, but he had a gut feeling that this trip might take longer than he'd have preferred, and he was a cautious man by nature. He wanted to be prepared for whatever lay ahead.

The flight had been—thankfully—brief and on time, and he soon found himself in line to pick up an Avis rental car. He grinned with pleasure as there was just one client ahead of him while the other rental agencies had huge lines. *Strange*, he thought. *There seems to be no rhyme or reason to this.* The simple fact was, he tended to be lucky a great deal of the time…

Hey, who's to question?

A quick survey of the map that the car rental provided showed that Sunningdale was an easy 30-minute drive. Soon he was pulling onto the grounds after passing through a rather impressive-looking pair of gates that opened to a large, imposing, multistoried building beyond. He was soon to discover a series of handsome cottages located around a small lake. He later learned that these cottages were called villas, which was a bit pretentious, *But hey, whatever sells*, he thought.

The map that was given to him at the gate showed the location of Laura's villa. *I wonder how much of the initial fee for this place has set Laura back, not to mention the yearly fees?* He later learned that his assessment of the sizable cost was dead on.

As Willis drove towards the entrance, he noted that the shrubbery was immaculately trimmed. A profusion of flowerbeds in an array of cheerful red and white geraniums led up to the entry. He soon reached the sizable, covered parking area that could easily hold a dozen or so cars at a time to shelter guests' cars during inclement weather. As he walked up to the front entry, he had to wait as a woman on a walker and an aide left the building before he could go through the glass doors and enter the lobby.

The lobby was richly furnished in soft beiges with accents of soothing blues. There were numerous plants (real, not fake), plus a huge arrangement of fresh flowers in yellows and whites with additional accents of blues from some iris, all arranged in a large, expensive-looking vase on a round wooden table, which had a rich inlaid border that ran around the edge of the table. This table commanded the center of the room and set a tone of elegance and taste that Willis was soon to learn was the main, desired theme of Sunningdale itself… rich, elegant, and serene.

The woman behind the front desk had a look that extended this impression of class and entitlement. She wore a cheerful outfit in yellows and beige and had a sunny disposition to match.

Willis walked up to the desk and smiling, she asked, "May I be of some help?"

"Yes" replied Willis, nodding his head. "I'm here to see Mrs. Wilk. I believe she's expecting me."

The woman nodded and said, "Yes, she certainly is. The

name is Inspector Willis, is it not?"

Willis nodded his agreement and she responded "I'll just let her know that you're here." She dialed a number and said, "Mrs. Wilk, that gentleman that you seemed so anxious to see has just arrived." After a brief pause, she said, "I'll send him right over."

The receptionist hung up and took out a map of Sunningdale and a yellow highlighter to mark out the direction for Willis to take. "Just follow the road to your right after you go out the front door and look for the sign that says 'Woodridge Colony.' Mrs. Wilks's villa is the fourth one on the left as you enter the drive, and it has the number 8 on it. You can't miss it. You can either drive or it's a rather pleasant walk," she said with a reassuring smile.

Willis said, "I think I'll drive over, as I have a few things in the car that would be difficult to carry." He then proceeded to return to his car and drive there, as Laura had suggested that he stay with her and he might as well drive there with his suitcase, etc. The etc. consisted of a beautiful, rather large flowering plant that he luckily had been able to pick up on his drive to Sunningdale.

Willis easily found the entrance to the Woodridge Colony and Laura's villa, and parked in one of the three spots marked "guests." Willis thought to himself, *My guess is that folks here don't have many visitors.* This later proved to be rather accurate.

Taking the flowering plant and his suitcase, he walked up the Willis path to Laura's home. Willis was keenly aware that a nearby neighbor was quietly observing his arrival as she walked her small dog. At one point, the dog tugged at his lead wanting to move on, but the neighbor was clearly more engrossed with seeing what was going on next door.

Willis had barely reached for the doorbell when the front door swung open and there stood Laura, the lady who had been his mother's best and most loyal friend. She was a handsome woman who, despite her being in her mid to late 50s, looked amazingly attractive and youthful in her bright pink pants with a pink and white patterned blouse to match.

Yes, thought Willis, *she basically looks the same when I last saw her.* But there was something missing and then he realized that Laura, who had always been so full of humor and warmth, stood there smiling but there was no real warmth in her expression. It was just a put-on mask without any heart and it disturbed Willis.

"Oh, Inspector, it's so good to see you. How can I ever thank you enough for coming here?" There was a slight pause, and Laura waved her hand across her face and said, "Oh, how silly of me. I meant to say 'Willis.' You're no longer attached to that detective department, are you?"

"No, Laura, I left the department a while ago and formed my own investigating company called 'The 3 in 1 Investigating Agency.' I have two wonderful partners, Monty and Ross Anderson, and the three of us have been amazingly busy and successful since we began our company. But I'm sure my mother told you that people out of habit still call me 'Inspector Willis.'"

Laura smiled and said, "Yes, of course, how foolish of me."

Willis smilingly handed her the plant and said, "Something to brighten up your day."

"Oh, it's so beautiful and cheery. Your mother always said how thoughtful you were. Thank you so much for this and for coming here on such short notice... Please, put your bag down over there, and let's sit and talk."

Willis quickly put his bag down as directed and followed Laura over to a table with two chairs which was obviously set for tea. Laura, upon hearing from the front desk that Willis had arrived at Sunningdale, had turned the kettle on and soon she produced a steaming pot of tea.

Willis looked at Laura with sort of a surprised curiosity. While he hardly knew her, he began to realize that while his mother had been 74 when she died, Laura was considerably younger, say maybe somewhere in her 50s. He then recalled that there had been quite an age difference between Laura and her husband. *Come to think of it, there's not much of an age difference between Laura and myself. She might be maybe four years or so years older than me,* he thought.

His musing was interrupted by Laura asking, "Would you prefer coffee or something stronger?"

"No, tea will be just fine," he replied. "I'm actually a big tea drinker."

And so, the two of them settled into having a rather formal tea, as there were little tea cakes on a three-level tiered dish that matched a very pretty tea set with teapot, cake dishes, teaspoons, and so forth. Laura might be upset, but she always had a reputation for being the perfect hostess.

Willis turned down the offer of the little cakes, but nodded when she gestured towards the tea itself. Having settled that bit of business, Willis asked, "Now what's this all about? You sounded very concerned about something and from what my mother used to say, that's not at all like you. What's going on?"

Laura took a sip of her tea, went to grab a piece of cake, changed her mind, and finally said, "I might be getting a bit paranoid, but I don't think so. There are some very strange things going on around here and it has me worried. No, make that frightened... very frightened."

"Please, tell me what's going on, Laura," Willis said as he put down his cup and leaned forward.

"Well, I'm not exactly sure where to begin. as something strange has been going on for a while now. Let me start at the beginning if, God forbid, it's just the beginning."

She paused, pursed her lips a bit, and then let out a sigh. "I arrived here about three years ago. I know you'll think that I'm rather young for being in a continuing care facility, but my husband was considerably older than me and we came here, probably more like three and a half years ago to think of it. As luck would have it, Herb had a massive heart attack and died shortly after we moved in, so here I am," she said with a wry look on her face.

"It's actually a good fit for me, as there are lots of activities and lots of interesting people. To be perfectly honest, this place is expensive, VERY expensive, and most people here have been successful and are really interesting to be with. Of course, there are a number of older people and, well, with age comes some failures... A heart attack here, a stroke there. Anyway, there was a man named Ralph Talmon who was the picture of health, hit the gym every day, was only 63 and suddenly he was dead! Some said it was a stroke, others said a heart attack, but whatever it was, it got him, and he was gone. There was a lovely memorial service for him. Rather a wonderful turnout… he was very popular, you see. But I don't… I just don't know… something just felt a little off to me. It just didn't seem right. But then I had a little talk with myself. I said, 'Now, Laura, you're just being a foolish old so-and-so. Quit drawing false conclusions.' And so, I kinda dropped the whole thing… Out of mind, you might say."

Willis smiled warmly at her, as she had so many of his mother's mannerisms… ways of expressing herself. And so, trying to encourage her, Willis said, "Go on, Laura."

"Well, it's kind of hard to explain, but there are some rather odd things occurring here that have me disturbed."

There was a long pause, and she finally went on to say, "Call me crazy, but people are dying here in strange and sudden ways. You know me, Willis, I'm like your mother, a sensible person who's not inclined to have wild or crazy thoughts, but something is amiss here and I'm determined to find a way to stop it."

Willis had to agree. While Laura was unique and prone to be opinionated, Willis knew from his mother that Laura certainly always made great sense in how she dealt with the people in her life and wasn't inclined to exaggerate or be an alarmist. And so, Willis carefully and gently said, "So what exactly do you mean by 'dying in strange and sudden ways'?"

Laura replied, "About three years ago, no, really two and a half years ago to be exact, I started playing Canasta with Helen Cronin, who lived several villas down from here. She was a devil at the game but drove me crazy at times." Laura looked briefly away, and then returning said, "She was darn charming but she cheated at cards. I hate that! Anyway, she had a cozy villa, much like the one I have here... Two bedrooms, kitchen, dining area, living room, and a small office. Really cute. It fit her perfectly, as she had a small family who occasionally visited her but not too often. She was religious about working out at the gym with that good-looking trainer we have here, she ate healthy foods, you know all the things they tell us we should do to have a healthy, full and long life."

"Well, to my knowledge, she had seldom had a sick day in her life and suddenly she was gone. Died just like that!" Laura punctuated the statement with a snap of her fingers. "Agnes, our cleaning lady, found her sprawled out on the floor in her gym clothes and the assumption was she had had a heart attack while exercising. The strange thing is, she never exercised at home. She always went to the gym, as she loved the camaraderie of her fellow gym buddies, especially that cute trainer, what's his name? Well, anyhow, Agnes wasn't sure what to do so she called the front desk, and someone immediately called Harry, the Sunningdale doctor on call and he did the usual thing… that is. pronounced her dead."

"The police soon arrived and did what policemen do I suppose... They took photos and so forth, then she was taken away. I don't know, it just didn't make sense. Then more strange things started to occur. Since then, two healthy, vital people I know have died suddenly, seemingly without cause. I know what you're thinking, this place is full of old people and old people die, but in all three cases, they were mentally alert, extremely healthy, and full of life. They weren't always the most charming or the nicest people but, I don't know... It just seems strange and alarming."

"Well, it all started to come to a head when..." Laura paused, as if she had heard someone or something that had interrupted her train of thought, and said, as she put down her teacup, "Excuse me. I think I heard something." She quickly went into the back bedroom and closed the door. There was silence, except for the sound of the back door slamming shut.

After a long pause, Laura entered the room looking very flustered. When Willis looked at her inquisitively, she brushed his questioning look aside and proceeded to tidy up her hairdo.

Having eventually settled down, Laura proceeded as if nothing had transpired by saying, "Now where were we? Oh yes, I know, some strange things are going on here, but maybe I'm talking out of turn. I don't know, it's all so confusing. Why don't we finish our tea, I can give you a key to the front door and you can get settled in. The guestroom is just down the hall there and please, if you need anything, just let me know."

Interesting, thought Willis, but he opted to put his

thoughts on hold. Soon he was in the guestroom and, as he unpacked, he looked around the room. It was a nice, very orderly room with a double bed, a dressing table with mostly empty drawers, a few assorted photos of family and friends along with a few crisply starched antimacassars on top of the chairs, which looked like the ones his mother used to make. In short, there were the usual expected items, except when Willis opened the closet to hang up his clothes, he saw there were a few outfits way in the back, mostly in dark grays or blacks which, from Willis's limited understanding, were colors Laura never wore. He remembered that his mother used to marvel at Laura's flair for mixing colors… *Always bright colors or pastels but never black or dark grays. Obviously, these belong to someone else…perhaps a house guest who visits frequently and left a few items.*

He casually wondered about this but didn't give it much thought as Laura knocked softly on the bedroom door. When Willis opened it, she said, "Sorry to disturb you, but I'm strangely tired and thought I'd take a liedown. How are you for drinks at 6:00? I know you New York types… Always have drinks and dinner on the late side. We normally have cocktails at 5 but in deference to you, I've moved things a bit later. I've invited a few friends over who I think you'll enjoy meeting. We can all go to the restaurant here at Sunningdale for dinner after drinks if that would suit you."

In response, Willis said, "I'd love to meet your friends, and drinks and dinner sound perfect. Have a nice rest."

She half-smiled as though there was a thought going on inside her head, nodded, and quietly closed the door leaving Willis to finish his unpacking.

At dusk, just before 5:00, Willis left his room and went for a walk. Besides Laura's home, there was a collection of villas surrounding the decorative pond which had a charming fountain in the middle. Off at one end was a tall white building that seemed to house the majority of the residents of Sunningdale. In the pond was a collection of waterfowl who, like some of the residents, had made the pond and the surroundings their home. There were five or six ospreys, a few pelicans, a small group of egrets, but mostly an assortment of ducks, including a pair that were mostly black but had bright red feathers about their heads... Very pretty and unusual. Willis nodded to a man sitting on a bench at the edge of the pond. He wore black slacks and a black and white plaid shirt and was feeding the birds with small pieces of bread that he tore off from the slices he carried in a small brown bag.

Willis said as he pointed to the birds, "How charming they all are!"

To which the man said, "Oh, we have many beautiful and charming birds here but those two over there," as he pointed to the two black and red feathered birds, "are greatly valued because they're really very rare. Did you know that they mate for life, which is exceptionally rare, especially around here?" he said with a wry chuckle... the inference being that many of the inhabitants at Sunningdale were on their second or third marriage. The man then said, "By the way, my name is Bruton Manchester. And you?"

Willis replied, "I'm Willis," and they shook hands and quietly watched the birds for a while. Finally, Bruton said, "Well, I best be going home. I don't much care to be out here in the dark despite the extensive lighting of the fountain and surrounding shoreline." They again shook hands and Willis watched as Bruton picked up his nearly finished bottle of water, took a swig, waved goodbye, and wandered off. Willis wasn't sure if the wave was directed toward him or toward the birds.

He stayed a while enjoying the view, but it was now becoming increasingly difficult for Willis to see, as the sun was rapidly setting. As he worked his way back to Laura's villa, he spotted a person in a neighboring yard who was all in black, including a hat that covered most of his face. Strangely, as far as Willis could see, the person appeared to be also wearing black gloves and it looked like he was brushing something onto the fruit of a lone tree that was about eight feet tall. Maybe he was fertilizing it, but Willis wasn't sure. He didn't think much of it as he glanced at his watch and realized Laura's cocktail guests would probably be arriving soon. He thought he'd best hightail it back to Laura's and maybe change into something fresh.

When he arrived, it dawned on him that Laura had not given him a key as promised, so he knocked softly on the door. There was a bit of a scuffle of noise and, eventually, Laura opened the door, looking a bit flustered.

"Oh, I'm so sorry. I totally forgot to give you a key. I'm afraid Harry, our Sunningdale doctor, is right when he teases me, saying that if my head wasn't screwed onto my shoulders, I'd lose it! Now I must set out the drinks and so forth to get ready for our guests. Will you give me a hand?"

Willis said, "Of course. What can I do to help?"

Gesturing towards a small bar set up near the couch, she said, "How about filling that ice bucket with ice from the freezer in the kitchen while I put out some things to nibble on?"

As Willis was busy getting ice into the ice bucket, he heard the doorbell ring and the sound of guests arriving. *So much for my changing clothes,* he thought.

Laura went to the front door and greeted two guests with "Hi! God it's great to see the two of you."

As they walked into the living room, Willis saw two ladies who could not be more dissimilar. The first lady was blonde and full of smiles. She was exceptionally pretty and beautifully turned out. She wore a soft, light green and lavender print dress, and as she walked forward to meet Willis, she exuded a confident air, the aura of someone who has had the privilege of people being predisposed to liking her before they ever engaged her in conversation. Willis also made note that she wore a very large diamond ring. He was soon to learn that her intelligence matched her good looks and good fortune.

The other woman was a festival of contrast to the first lady. She had gray, unkempt hair that was cut in an unbecoming pageboy style and wore no makeup. As far as Willis could see, she was a woman who didn't pay much attention to her appearance. She simply looked disorganized, a bit disheveled, and obviously not interested in what she looked like. Being a bit overweight didn't help matters.

Laura placed her arm around the good-looking lady and directed her towards Willis, saying, "I want you to meet Felicia Ross. She and I have been good friends ever since I moved in here. We met over a game of canasta in the community card room and clicked from the very beginning. Didn't we, Felicia?"

Felicia nodded with a dazzling smile, took Willis's hand,

and greeted him with, "It's wonderful to finally meet you." Meanwhile, Laura pulled the other lady over and introduced her as Matty, Matty King. She appeared to be more serious and less inclined to smile. She was nevertheless polite and proved interesting in her own way. Her handshake was quite firm, and while she exuded considerable intelligence, any trace of charm had clearly forsaken her.

Felicia forged ahead, saying, "Laura has told us quite a bit about you, Inspector. As you now know, my name is Felicia. How do you prefer to be addressed? As 'Inspector Willis' or just plain Willis?"

"Oh, please, Felicia, call me Willis, even though everyone continues to call me 'Inspector Willis'. The Inspector title comes from my days in the police force but that was in another life," he said with a charming smile. "I'm now a private investigator and happy to be my own man.

"Fair enough," said Felicia.

Meanwhile, the other lady appeared to stand in Felicia's shadow. She slouched, which added to the drabness of her overall appearance as her clothing was also devoid of color. Her one asset, Willis was later to learn, was she had a sharp intelligence, which resulted in her having keen observation skills. This, however, did not extend to her having any trace of social graciousness. In short, she was both sharp and dull.

Willis was instantly charmed and fascinated with both

ladies. He immediately decided to learn more about the two of them.

Laura, being the perfect hostess, suggested that everyone take a seat in the living room. Willis pulled out a chair for Felicia, and before he could do the same for Matty, the latter had plopped down in one of the chairs, causing it to slide away from the coffee table and land her at an awkward angle. She noisily slid her chair back to its logical location. Willis later learned that Matty was a wizard when it came to computers. She often helped Laura who, while socially skilled, was less than talented when it came to computer skills.

As everyone got settled in, Laura asked, "What would everyone like? I'm having a kir but I have most everything," to which Felicia asked for "just a glass of white wine, no *creme de cassis,*" which showed somewhat her knowledge of drinks. When Marty hesitated to place an order, Willis went to the bar and poured Felicia her winc and a scotch rocks for himself. Matty finally said, "Oh white wine will do. Can I have a few ice cubes in it please?"

When everyone had settled in, Felicia said, "Did anyone see that person who seemed to be fussing with Claudine Hollar's fruit tree? He was all in a very dark outfit. All very strange and not typical of folks around here and at this hour!"

"Oh, Claudine and that damn tree of hers. She seems so

obsessed with it," said Matty.

"Well it is rather unique," said Laura. "After all, it isn't every day one sees a tree that has been grafted to have one branch with lemons, another with peaches, and a third with oranges, and oh, how she dotes on the peach branch especially.

"Anyway," said Felicia, "I wonder what that's all about. I guess Claudine hired someone to either fertilize or maybe protect the plant from bugs."

"No, can't say that I saw anyone, but then I tend not to delve into other people's business," said Matty "Oh, I'm sorry Felicia, that came out all wrong. It sounded like I was accusing you of being a busybody." Which, of course, was exactly what she was intimating.

"Oh, I understand. By the way, someone said you were looking for a good hairdresser, Matty. Have you looked into that new shop in St. Armand's Circle called 'A Cut Away Hair Salon'? You might want to try it."

Matty subconsciously ran her hand through her hair, making it more of a mess than it had been, but for a change didn't say a word.

Laura nodded her approval, but it wasn't clear who she was agreeing with. She went on to say, "Have any of you heard any word if Claudine is going to go with us to the concert next Friday? It's a group of singers from Yale's Chorus who give concerts during their class breaks and over the holidays. They're supposed to be quite good."

"I'm not sure," said Felicia. "But I can stop by her place tomorrow and ask her. As you know, she never answers her phone."

"Why's that?" asked Willis.

"Search me," replied Felicia.

"Oh," said Laura, "I think she's just very introverted... Not a social person. Not very interested in others, although the other day she gossiped a bit, saying that she was adamant that she knew something VERY important and that she was planning to go to Carl Stoner, you know the man who basically runs this place, and make him aware of something strange that's going on here at Sunningdale."

"Any idea what that could be, Laura?" asked Willis.

"I don't know, but she seemed inordinately distressed over whatever it was that she wanted to discuss with Carl. Not like her at all."

"Odd," said Felicia.

To which Matty said, "Maybe I'll stop by her place tomorrow and try to find out what she's concerned about."

"Good idea," said Felicia, while Laura looked a bit concerned.

Willis asked Laura, "Do you think we could all go over together and see what this is all about? Would that be ok with you, Matty?"

"Fine," she said with a shrug. "I'm sure it's nothing, but why not be prudent and make sure."

Laura looked skeptical but shrugged, indicating her willingness to go along with the idea.

And so, after a while the three ladies and Willis finished their drinks and headed over for dinner at Sunningdale's main restaurant, The Westwind, which turned out to be smart but not overly formal, with the clientele either in dressy casual attire or in some cases a bit dressier. The men were either in slacks and a collared shirt, the minimum requirement, or a sports jacket typically without a tie and the women wore either handsome dresses or dress slacks. Laura was wearing an elegant sea-green dress that matched her eyes and a beautiful diamond necklace and earring set that while eye-catching, was not ostentatious. Willis was enchanted with her.

They entered the bar area where they confirmed their dinner reservation, but decided not to have drinks around the bar, as Felicia encouraged everyone to have cocktails at their table, which had a beautiful view of the pond and its fountain. Laura made a point of suggesting that Willis take a certain chair that had "a great view," and everyone took a seat, unfolded their napkins, and settled in.

It turned out that Troy was their waiter, which seemed

to delight the ladies as he was clearly one of their favorites. He sported a rather large dirty-blonde ponytail, and one could see a bit of a tattoo on his left wrist which hinted at the potential of a lot more farther up. When he asked if anyone cared for a drink, it was made clear to him that each lady as usual intended to pay her own bill with Laura picking up the check for Willis despite Willis's objection. Apparently, there had been a choice of three restaurants, and at a quiet moment Laura whispered in Willis's ear that this was the better of the three. "It's more elegant, has a more interesting menu, and…" she said with a sly smile and a wink, "Troy works here."

The ladies chatted away with Felicia making a point of including Willis in the conversation. They soon ordered drinks that reflected what they drank earlier. The conversation was easy and lively with most of the conversation revolving around some gossip about Elise, one of the more dominant members of Sunningdale who was causing a bit of a ruckus with the other members of her colony over the art in their common room.

When it came time to order, Felicia ordered the salad as she was, as usual, on a diet, although her "diet" didn't seem to extend to the calories in her drink consumption. Matty ordered the prime rib "Rare but not too rare, and can I have something other than the string beans as they were overcooked last time and were just this side of mush. Oh, and yes, be sure to give me some horseradish on the side, please." She did this as she reached for yet another piece of cornbread from the breadbasket.

Laura seemed undecided, but finally gave in and said, "I'll have the same as Matty." Willis, after some deliberation followed by asking for some suggestions from the ladies, ended up choosing the "Seafood Plate" which he was told was "one of the better dishes available here." Troy was used to these sorts of decisions and the occasional bits of indecision. Shortly, he came back with another basket that contained a selection of breads "Just for you special ladies," which he said with a wink. Matty dove into the basket, taking another large piece of cornbread. The rest made other choices except for Felicia, who again made it clear that she was dieting.

Over drinks, Matty proceeded to ask Willis, "So what's your first impression of Sunningdale?"

Willis replied, "Well since I just got here, I can't say that I've formed a conclusive impression, but so far I find the place extremely handsome, and yes, I'd say comfortable in that the front desk was welcoming and efficient. The homes around the lake are quite attractive... very charming, as are the few inhabitants who I've met so far." He said this with a little salute of his drink which charmed the ladies.

Felicia especially smiled in return and asked if he was, in fact, checking out the place as a possible home for himself and his wife sometime in the near future. The question that really had been asked was, of course "Is he married?" When he made it clear that he was divorced, there was a moment of silence as each woman processed the reply and possibly planned her next move.

Over dinner, the subject of the deaths of several occupants came up, but the subject was quickly brushed aside by Laura with the excuse that she didn't want to give Willis the wrong impression about Sunningdale, to which the ladies quickly agreed. However, later over dessert, the subject of Roz's passing came up and it became apparent that Laura wasn't the only person concerned about this odd death at Sunningdale.

When it came time for dessert, everyone passed except Matty, and when she ordered the *crème brulée*, the rest relented and each ordered the same, all except Felicia, who said, "I'm sticking to my regimen: come hell or high water, no desserts until I lose five pounds."

And so, the dinner concluded, and everyone said their good nights, with the ladies enthusiastically saying they hoped to see "more of Willis." When Laura and Willis returned alone to her villa, they settled in on the veranda overlooking the pond with another glass of Pinot for Laura and a light scotch rocks for Willis.

As Willis took his first sip, Laura asked him, "How's work going for you?"

"Do you mean regarding your concern here or in general?"

"Oh, both. While I'm of course interested in how your life is going on in general, I'm certainly very interested in the impression you had tonight with regard to what Felicia and Matty had to say."

"Okay, as to your first question, work in general with my two assistants Ross and Monty couldn't be better. We have the pleasure of solving problems and mysteries and we appear to be very good at it. Funny, I always thought I was a smart, insightful inspector when I was on the force, but now that I'm on my own, along with Ross and Monty, I find that I'm more focused and, in some ways, more perceptive. I believe I've really found my niche, Laura, and that feels really good."

Strangely, as if I'm not busy enough, I've been concerned about buiding up my portfolio, you know, my reserves. So I've started buying properties, one at a time and the boys, Monty and Ross, have joined forces with me. As a team we're doing amazingly well with flipping houses, you know buying them on the cheap side, fixing them up so they look really nice and then selling them for a profit. We're just in the early stages but we seem t,o have a knack for this… A really pleasant surprise."

Laura tilted her head as she took in this new piece of information. *This man is full of surprises*, she thought.

Willis, who tended to not share his deeper thoughts, turned the conversation back towards Laura by asking, "Did anything strike you as odd this evening? What's your take on what the ladies said regarding strange things happening here?"

"Oh, I don't know, Willis. Part of me wants to know if, in fact, something terribly wrong is going on and another part of me says 'Laura, just relax and let things go. You're just being ridiculous. With that, she polished off her glass of Pinot Grigio and looked longingly at the bottle but shook her head, smiled, and said, "I'd best head for bed as it's been a very full day for me thanks to you. Please let me know if you need anything."

Willis smiled and said, "I'm ok for now. See you in the morning. I think I'll stay up for a while and review things a bit."

Laura smiled, gave him a mock salute, and said, "Good night then Inspector. Sleep well." She went into her room, leaving Willis with a smile on his face.

After a while, Willis took a final sip of his drink, carried the glass to the kitchen, rinsed it, and left it on the counter by the dishwasher. He was soon in his room and, after brushing his teeth in the small but efficient bathroom, crawled into bed. But sleep was apparently not on his schedule. He stared at the ceiling and mulled things over: *Something's odd here and I just can't put my finger on it, but hopefully in time...*

Friday—Day Three
Laura and some of her friends

Willis got up at 7:30, which was a bit late for him, as he had always been a very early riser, but he found staying up late reviewing the evening with the three ladies and trying to figure out what was happening here in Sunningdale exhausting. Making sense of the situation seemed to him like trying to nail Jell-O to the wall. And so, he got up, brushed his teeth, took a shower, shaved, and got dressed for the day.

While most of the gentlemen at dinner had worn jackets, Willis surmised that a nice long-sleeved shirt and slacks would work just fine for daytime wear, and it turned out that he was right on. He went into the kitchen, poured a cup of coffee into a mug Laura had thoughtfully set out, and walked out to the back terrace. Laura soon followed him. She was wearing a white belted terrycloth bathrobe, carrying her own cup of coffee. She said, "Good morning, Willis. Did you sleep okay?"

"Like a baby. That's a very comfortable bed in there." He gestured towards the guestroom.

She nodded and said, "Glad to hear it." She then took a watering can and carefully and very gently started to water a beautiful, small bonsai tree growing in a deep red Asian-shaped pot on a nearby table.

"That's a beautiful plant you have there. Is it new?"

"Oh no, it's actually quite old. Mark, a very close friend of mine, collected bonsai trees and gave this one to me just before he died. I really love it and I take great care of it. It's my way of keeping Mark alive... at least the love and affection I felt for him. I find it very beautiful and it reminds me of that wonderful friendship I had. I so love it! Do you know anything about bonsai trees, Willis?"

"No, can't say that I do."

"Well, briefly, bonsai trees are miniature trees that are generally planted in decorative trays or pots, often with pebbles arranged around them. They originated from the Chinese practice of penjing and were then adapted by the

Japanese to decorate their homes. Because of the small sizes of these plants, they need to be carefully taken care of. I move it indoors and out depending on the weather, and I water this beautiful tree every day, as it must never dry out. I love it. It's my baby!"

After watering it, she smiled, grabbed her cup of coffee, and, giving Willis a little wave, went back to her part of the house. In a remarkably short time, to Willis's amazement, she reappeared fully transformed in lavender slacks and shoes plus a blouse that had a pink and lavender pattern that matched her slacks perfectly. Willis noticed that she had removed the diamond bracelet and earrings set she had worn the previous evening and had replaced them with a simple pair of earrings and ring set with amethyst stones that matched the lavender in her outfit.

What remained on her at all times was a large diamond ring that was just over five carats, which had reportedly been given to her by her late husband Hal as a 25th wedding anniversary gift when they were on a safari in Kenya. She initially was thrilled with the ring, but felt ill at ease about being out in a tent in "the middle of nowhere", surrounded by many strangers, so she reluctantly turned the stone in toward the palm of her hand, thereby hiding the stone from view. When she returned from their trip, she took to wearing the ring so the stone showed prominently. She eventually grew to think of it as an extension of her whole being. She continued to wear it even after Hal had passed away, and to everyone's knowledge the ring had never been removed except once, when she had some surgery—which some secretly thought might have been a facelift.

Willis had always known that Laura had excellent taste, but her look this morning was just short of spectacular and he let out a low-keyed appreciative whistle.

Laura grinned like a young girl at the whistle, and he noted that on rare occasions she showed a faint sign of having dimples, which made her look years younger. She was charming and certainly beautiful. Willis had heard his mother say that Laura had been a great beauty in her youth, so much so that a photo of her once appeared on the cover of *Life Magazine*. A man named Hal Ward, who was highly successful in the aluminum extrusion business, saw the photo and tracked her down. Apparently, when he saw Laura's photo, he had decided then and there that she was the woman he wanted to share the rest of his life with and that's exactly what happened.

They were married for 29 years before he died of a massive heart attack while climbing in the Dolomites in Italy. Willis's mother said the marriage lasted because Hal traveled so much that neither one got on each other's nerves. Hal used to say that Laura was a combination of so many different women and that he always loved coming home to see "which one he was married to this time." This latter part fascinated Willis.

The two sat there deep in their own thoughts. Willis reminisced about his mother and said, "When I was quite young, my mother, who was a marvelous, very perceptive woman, sat me down and said, 'You can be anything you want to be. All you need to do is focus on a dream and then go for it!' She was amazing! Somehow, she saw a potential in me that I never knew existed. Her faith in me gave me the courage and drive to realize the potential that had been there all the time. I truly am the man I am today thanks to that marvelous woman… I was extraordinarily lucky!"

Laura was beginning to discover what a special man he was…to date she had just seen the tip of the iceberg.

She was brought out of her reverie when Willis said, "I have some calls I need to make to my boys about a house we just bought to fix up. It's a challenging project but one that we are all very 'up' on. What are the plans for the day?"

Laura replied that she typically went over to help her friend Rebecca first thing in the morning. It seems that Rebecca had an electric tricycle which she rode daily, until one day she misjudged a turn she was making and hit a mailbox with such force that she ended up with a broken collarbone and a fractured right arm. Unfortunately,

Rebecca was right-handed, and it was expected that she would be incapacitated for a considerable length of time.

Laura was understandably concerned for her friend, so she made it a practice to visit Rebecca most mornings to help her with chores, like brushing her hair and washing it when needed, writing emails for her, and so forth. She also did Rebecca's food shopping, which was no big deal as Laura did Rebecca's shopping when she went to the store for her own needs. She explained this to Willis so he would understand when she was gone for an hour or two each morning.

This particular day, it was agreed that after Laura returned from going over to Rebecca's, that she and Willis would pick up Felicia and Matty at the Club at 11:00 AM and head over to Claudine's.

Claudine lived in a villa near the North Tower. She had a fantastic view of the water, a charming mini-garden with her prized plants, including, as Laura had mentioned earlier, a special tree that had been grafted so that it had a branch with oranges, another with peaches, and one with lemons. Claudine not only loved her garden, she was also very fond of her villa and took great pride in the display of the many treasures that she had acquired on her numerous travels overseas, including many Asian works of art… wood carvings and wall hangings. She particularly avoided any carvings made out of ivory, as she was adamant about her dislike of killing elephants for their ivory. Any mention of the subject would cause her to go on a long lecture to anyone present about the evils of such treatment of animals, especially elephants.

Like Laura, she was a widow and had been slowly trying to work her way into one of the other residents' lives. His name was Bruton, and whenever she saw him feeding the ducks, she would magically show up and try to engage him in conversation, unfortunately with little or no success to date. Perhaps the rumors that Bruton was gay were true. No one knew for sure. Laura later confided that she found out that Claudine had gotten on Bruton's nerves to the point that he was trying to find a way to distance himself from her. He might just have encouraged the idea that he was gay to turn her off. Such was some of the interplay that took place at Sunningdale.

When the ladies finally got to Claudine's villa, they rang her doorbell but there was no response.

"That's odd," said Felicia. "I spoke with her just before we said good night at the restaurant last night and I'm sure she's expecting us." Felicia looked at her watch and said, "Yup, it's eleven on the dot. I'm sure we said eleven."

"I wonder if we should go in to make sure she's ok," said Matty.

"Well, I happen to have a key to her place on me, since I often water her plants when she's out of town," said Laura as she dug into her purse and produced a key. She unlocked the door and led the ladies and Willis into Claudine's home. At first, everything seemed normal.

Matty called out, "Claudine, are you here?" When there was no answer, the ladies began to look through the apartment. Laura was the first to find Claudine's body on the floor of the far side of the large bed in the master bedroom. It was soon clear that she was dead and Willis quickly called 911 while Matty took out her cell phone and called Carl Stone at his office. When told of Claudine's death he replied, "I'll be right over. Matty, did you call 911?"

"No. I was going to, but Willis beat me to it."

So the ladies waited nervously while quietly discussing what could have happened.

When the paramedics arrived, they discovered an empty bottle of melatonin pills with the label partially torn off in one of her pockets. The police were immediately called.

Two officers soon arrived. The taller of the two policemen questioned each lady, as well as Willis. The police inspector wanted to know if Claudine had been depressed or had suicidal thoughts. Each of the ladies adamantly said, "No!" Not that they knew of. This whole thing was a mystery to everyone.

Eventually, after the police took numerous photos, Claudine's body was taken away in an ambulance and the ladies sadly drifted back to their various homes. However, before Willis left, he spotted a bowl of peaches and quietly took one. When he got back to Laura's, he called a buddy of his and arranged that he would take the peach and deliver it to the guy's lab to have it analyzed. Willis explained to Laura that he had some emergency business to take care of and that he would be gone for two or three hours.

When he brought the peach to a lab, he was told that it would take maybe a week or so to get the results. Willis then explained what his former career had been and it was agreed that as a special favor and out of respect for his former position as an inspector, they would get the results to him in a day or two. *Nice that my former title still gives me a little pull,* he thought. *I wonder how long that pull will last?*

Later that afternoon when he had returned to Laura's, she suggested that he might enjoy having dinner with a few more of her friends, to which he readily agreed. It turned out her friends lived in the Tower, the large building near the pond that housed a series of venues including a lecture hall, a small shop that carried snacks, greeting cards and such, a computer center where folks could get technical help, several restaurants, and a snack bar that offered hamburgers, hot dogs, and pizzas, among other things. These venues took up the first floor.

In the lobby was a bank of elevators that took people to the apartments above. On the various levels, there were groups of apartments located each around a handsome "common room," which typically was about 35 feet by 35 feet with tall ceilings, maybe 20 feet high. and the surrounding group of apartments formed what was referred to as a "colony", each with a name of its own. The colony Laura and Willis went to was called "The Willows."

It was agreed that Laura and Willis would have cocktails at Shelia Sullivan's, and then go on to dinner at the Pour House, one of the three restaurants at Sunningdale's. They arrived at Shelia's after an inordinate wait for an elevator. While they waited, Laura explained to Willis, "While Sunningdale is an amazingly well-run organization, one of the few really irritating aspects of the Tower is the seeming lack of sufficient elevator banks to handle the numerous residents. Shelia, who we're visiting, calls it 'A golden problem' but only when she's not in a rush." Laura punctuated the statement with a roll of her eyes.

Laura went on to explain, "Shelia's been married twice. Her first husband was a real loser named Larry Holbrook, who was a nightmare. They had two boys and he had a bad habit of getting his points across with his hands. A slap here, a punch there. Late one night, after he had again beaten her up, she waited a while and finally woke up the kids, who were seven and nine at the time, took them into the bathroom, and showed how bruised and cut she was from the beatings Larry had given her."

"She wanted the kids to understand why she was planning to divorce him and take the boys away to a new life. The older boy understood, but the younger pleaded with her not to do it and so she reluctantly relented. However, the next time Larry used his fists to make a point, she didn't consult anyone. She packed up the boys and moved out, got a good lawyer, and finally a court order to keep Larry away. While building her divorce case, she went on the internet and discovered that Larry had a record of 'hit and runs' and an assault with a deadly weapon. To support herself and the boys, she took a job at a pharmacy, which is where she and I met. I was working there to help pay my way through college."

"Anyway, a few years later Shelia met a great guy named Carl Anderson. What a difference! He was highly successful and adored Shelia and the boys. They were married for sixteen years but, unfortunately, he developed cancer, a fast-moving one, and Shelia is now single again, but thank God, quite well off. The boys went on to college and are now out on their own. It'll be interesting to see what's in her next chapter, as she's a pistol and always up for another adventure."

They reached her door, rang the bell, and the door opened to reveal a very attractive older lady who was perfectly made up, and wore a matching sweater and skirt in navy blue with red trim which matched her lipstick and framed her large, inviting smile.

As they passed through the door, Laura said, "Shelia, meet Inspector Willis. Oh, I keep forgetting to drop the 'Inspector' part. Willis is the son of Rose who, as you know, was one of my dearest friends and he's here to help me solve a problem I'm having."

As they shook hands, Shelia gestured for them to come in. "Make yourselves comfortable," she said as she gestured towards the sofa. As they settled in, she said, "I'm having a martini. What can I get the two of you?"

"If you have some wine open, I would love a glass of white," said Laura, looking over to Willis.

He nodded and said, "That would be fine with me, too."

To which Shelia said, "Done" and proceeded to take a cold bottle of Pinot Grigio out of the bar refrigerator.

"Pinot okay with the two of you?" she asked. And upon a reply of nodding heads in approval, she efficiently opened the bottle. They had just taken their first sip when the doorbell rang. Shelia jumped up and said, "Oh, I forgot to mention, I've invited a few others, including Hal Snyder. I hope that's OK with you?" she said, directing her question to Laura. I just heard that the other two are running a bit late.

"Oh sure, I hardly know Hal but from what I know and have seen, he's a lovely man. However, I just heard that he had some disconcerting news. I hope it doesn't ruin the evening."

Shelia opened the door and there stood Hal Snyder, who made for a rather imposing sight in that he was six feet three or four and, unlike many men of that height, he was perfectly proportioned and had obviously kept himself in shape. While very attractive, he had a disturbed look on his face that would be there the entire evening. With him was a cute little woman dressed in black shorts and a western-type shirt in black, maroon, and burnt orange. Kind of an odd look.

Hal, without waiting for Shelia to make the introductions, said, "Hi everyone, I'm Hal Snyder and this here is Glo, Glo Siegman. She and I have been in an intense discussion all day and she's been incredibly supportive about a problem that's come up that I hate facing alone. I hope it's ok that I brought her along," he said, directing his last thought towards Shelia. As he said this, he slowly crossed the room, shook hands with everyone, and when Shelia asked him what he would like to drink, he replied, "Oh something non-alcoholic. Just water will be fine."

Looking at Glo, Shelia asked, "And what can I get you, dear?"

To which Glo said, "I see that you're all drinking white wine so that'd be fine with me, but can I have a little ice with it please?"

"Coming up," said Shelia, and she was soon back with another glass of white wine, some ice on the side, and water for Hal.

"On the way over, I happened to see a Buick in your driveway, Laura. Is that new?" asked Hal.

"No, that belongs to Willis here, who's staying with me."

Willis said, "It's ok for a rental, but I'd never buy one. It's just too loose, if you know what I mean. I like a car that responds quickly and this one is kind of 'on the sluggish side' if that makes sense."

"Oh, I know what you mean," piped up Glo. "Of course, I'm no expert when it comes to cars. All I know is I either like a car or I don't. Years ago, I had the most wonderful Volkswagen Beetle. God, I loved that car and drove it for ages."

"What happened to it?" asked Hal. "I've never seen you drive one."

Glo kind of giggled and said, "Well, it's sort of a long story but here goes...It's really a true story. As I said, I loved that car. She was so beautiful. Red with a tan interior. I called her Little Red. I drove her everywhere, including two trips cross-country. Well, one day I went to get her to drive to work, I lived in New York City at the time and as I said I drove her everywhere. Well, when I went to where I had parked on 54th and 7th Avenue, she was gone! I'm sure I parked her there but you know, after parking it in so many different places on the West Side over time, I thought, *Well, you're just confused Glo. Better check some other streets.* So, I hailed a cab and had the driver take me up and down the surrounding blocks... No sight of her! I consequently reported her stolen to the police, filled out a report, you know the drill, or maybe you don't."

"Anyway, I waited and waited for a call saying that she had been found, but nothing. After, say six weeks, I had pretty much given up all hope when I got a call from a policeman saying that the car I described with the license plate number I had given them had been found and if I went to a certain address in Brooklyn, I could claim it, but I should be sure to bring my license, and so forth for identification. So, I took the subway out to Brooklyn and when I got off the train, I walked about six or so blocks to a large fenced-in parking lot with what looked like hundreds of cars. I went through the entry gate up to a shed-like office and asked about my car."

"The policeman, who was very nice, went through sheet after sheet of paperwork and finally found the record of my car. He then turned to a fellow cop and said, 'I'm going to show this little lady her car. Hold down the fort, will ya?' and off we went. We went down row after row of a wild selection of cars until we finally found mine. There she was all dented, the roof lining was torn and hanging down, the upholstery was ripped, she was incredibly filthy! And I started to shake violently. The cop took pity on me and tried to comfort me. What he didn't realize was I was shaking with laughter. My beloved Little Red was exactly as I had left it when I parked it six weeks before, but now it had a new Blaupunkt radio in it!"

"Everyone laughed and said things like, 'I should be so lucky', and so forth."

Laura looked thoughtful and then said, "Ah, if only solutions were that easy and rewarding. Actually, in the long run, they were for me as I kinda moved on, met Randy, the love of my life, and just before he passed away, he surprised me for my birthday with a wonderful old 1996 Rolls Royce… It was creamy white with wonderful tan leather and burled wood detailing. God, I love that car and I will love that man forever!"

Willis looked at Laura and couldn't help smiling. He wanted to probe deeper into Laura's worries, but he felt that he had best do it privately later at a quiet moment. What or who was ruining her life? Did she have any idea who was causing her all this distress? He hoped that she might open up as to what her real concerns were. What suddenly amazed him was that he was starting to take an unusually deep concern for her well-being. It was now more than just helping a friend of his mother's. Were they entering a new stage in their friendship and where would it take them? Willis was suddenly very excited about the idea.

With that The doorbell rang and Shelia let in two more guests: a smartly dressed older woman who was impeccably coiffed, and an even older gentleman who Willis was later to find out was 96 years old.

"Everyone, if you don't already know these two, this beautiful lady is Else Carning, and her companion for this evening," she said with a wink and a smile, "is Anthony Stewart, our favorite doctor. While Anthony, or Tony as most folks call him, retired as a General Physician years ago, he never was able to break his habit of constantly keeping up with the latest medical information. His mind is as sharp as ever. He's very inquisitive, has a wonderful sense of humor, and is delighted with life itself." Everyone seemed charmed by the introduction, but Tony waved it off, although it was clear that he was delighted by the introduction.

Soon, Willis found himself sitting next to Tony and while it was evident that Tony had a few old age props such as hearing aids and a cane, he seemed devoid of any of the many attributes that seemed to haunt others much younger than himself, such as lapses in one's memory or any dis-association with life itself. While Willis chatted away with Tony, there was never a hesitant moment in his speech pattern. He was incredibly sharp.

Willis was fascinated by this man and soon asked Tony how long he had been in Sunningdale. Tony beamed and said, "My wife and I arrived here oh, I guess it was 22 years ago. No, make that 23. I remember because it was Alice's 70th birthday and we had the entire family here for a wonderful celebration." Tony stared off in the distance and said, "Alice and I were married 51 years at the time. We were together for a total of 74 years when she left me. She was a wonderful woman and I know it's silly, but I kiss her every morning… Well, her photo, in any case," he said with a grin.

"She helped put me through medical school, as we were quite poor in those days. It was a hard time for us, but we were young and in love and she had great faith in me. Together we built my practice as she worked as my receptionist until we started having our kids. It was a wonderful marriage, truly beautiful, and as a result, we had three children, with seven grandchildren, and now twelve great-grandkids... An even dozen!"

"As to our ending up here in Sunningdale, it was the

perfect move for us. Totally Alice's doing, as she was always the one to be prepared for whatever came down the pike. In our case, it was old age and Sunningdale has been a perfect security blanket. It's an institution that helps to keep one young and, of course, safe. You'd think it was just the medical team here but it's the residents too who are a big part of the support team. For example: your friend Laura. She is so attentive and helpful in getting me to my eye doctor's appointments. She's just wonderful!"

As Tony talked, he seemed very alert as to what was going on around him and suddenly took Willis's hand and, pointing to a mark on Willis's arm, said, "Young man, you should have that looked over. I might be wrong, but I suspect that you have a melanoma there which, unless you have it checked, could be a lot of trouble. Skin cancer is nothing to ignore or fool around with. Have a doctor look at it and stay out of the sun."

Willis smiled, because his GP had pointed it out a few months earlier and he had promised himself that he would check it out one of these days soon, but he had been so busy!

To get off the subject, Willis said, "I bet you've seen a lot here in Sunningdale... So many people each with his or her own joys and concerns."

"You certainly have that right, son," he said with a tap

on Willis's knee. You'd be surprised about what I see going on around here. As a matter of fact, I hear that Laura brought you here because of some concerns she has. You might find that what she's worried about may appear to be a bit farfetched, but I'd take her concerns seriously if I were you. This is not the place or time to get into that, but maybe we could have lunch or a drink and go over a few things I've noticed around here."

When he mentioned "a drink" there was a twinkle in his eye as though maybe they were sharing a secret. It was kind of a sweet yet poignant moment, and Willis decided to try to spend some time with Tony, as it might make for a charming time and, in truth, might well be a source for some important information.

In any case, the conversation between the two men was broken when Shelia placed her hand on Willis's arm and said, "I'm sorry to break up this intense conversation between the two of you, but I'd like you to meet Else... Else Carning. I think you two will find each other very interesting."

Willis found himself looking into the most intense blue eyes he had ever seen. Else was one of those people who looked at you with such a directness that one felt that one was looking into her very soul... or was it the other way around?

Willis took Else's hand and shook it, and at the same

time marveled at the strength of her grip. Clearly, she was a very strong, alert woman. Willis was later to find out that she had been one of the top interior decorators in the country and had many spreads in the top interior design magazines over the past two decades or so until she retired. She had been at the top of her game when her husband Patrick announced that they had best get settled into Sunningdale as soon as possible, as his twin brother was diagnosed with early-stage Alzheimer's. Fearful that he might suffer the same disability as his twin, he wanted both himself and Else to be safe and secure. Since neither of them had any family to speak of, it made great sense to have a place like Sunningdale to fall back on.

"Someday," said Else, "I'll tell you about my life, as it is quite interesting and surprising... At least it certainly has been for me," she said with a twinkle in her eyes.

While Willis contemplated this thought, Shclia broke in by asking Hal if he had any news from the doctors.

Everyone looked at Hal, and after a long pause, he said, "I'm afraid the news is bad, actually quite shocking, at least to me. Some of you know that I've been having some heart issues. Well, the doctors want me to have a heart transplant... a HEART TRANSPLANT! Very scary and confusing. I'm just now getting into it... To deal with this as it's all so complicated and scary."

There was again a long period of silence until he said, "From what I'm able to comprehend, there are four stages I'll need to go through before I can qualify to have the operation and get a new heart. That information doesn't cover subjects like who will care for me for the year after the transplant is completed, plus that cost and so forth. My understanding is it will cost over a million and a half dollars, nor have I gotten into fully knowing the prep and recovery stages. From my limited knowledge to date, I would be, as I said, into at least one year of recovery and would always be under the threat of having my body reject the new heart. That is, if they can find a heart that's compatible with my body. Unfortunately for every four people who have reached the stage where they qualify to get a transplant, there is only one heart available."

"Apparently, there have been several attempts to use hearts from pigs that were genetically adapted for humans, but the survival rate appears to be pretty dismal, so, no thank you to that idea! There's strangely a part of me that says okay, you're probably going to be dead very soon, why don't you just go out and do everything you've always wanted to do… both good and maybe even bad." With that he gave a kind of evil grin. "Maybe get even with someone I despise or make a sacrifice to help someone. I don't know. I'm so conflicted… I'm inundated with so many crazy thoughts. I wonder how the rest of you would handle this."

There was dead silence for a long time, then, "I wonder," thought Shelia out loud and perhaps a bit tactlessly. "If I were in your shoes with such a death threat hanging over my head, would I be reckless and do anything I wanted knowing that my time was limited? Just curious."

"Oh, I would certainly get my life in order," said Glo.

There was much discussion on the subject, even with someone comparing an old car with a new sound system and a failing body with a new engine. This joke, if it was a joke, didn't go over very well. In fact, the get-together got sort of heavy and lost its sense of fun and spontaneity, and people soon opted to leave.

On the way back to Laura's, she and Willis agreed that they had eaten so many *hors d'oeuvres* that neither was really very hungry. Instead, they sat for a while, with Willis checking his phone messages and Laura writing in her journal. Suddenly as if by telepathy, their hands touched and they sat there holding hands, and it felt good for both of them. In any case, Willis thought that whatever problem or problems Laura was having, they couldn't compare to the difficult one that Hal was facing. Little did Willis realize how far off he was from that truth.

Saturday—Day Four
There's a killer out there

Early that morning Willis found Laura out on the back terrace tenderly watering her beloved bonsai tree. He noted the extraordinary delicate twists and turns of its small miniature trunk, its intricate leaf arrangement, and the beautiful Asian-looking pot that housed the plant. The plant was a living piece of sculpture. Clearly, this plant meant a great deal to her.

Having finished her daily watering of the plant, she sat down on a nearby chaise and commenced to read the *New*

York Times and drink a mug of coffee. Like the morning before, she was in her white terrycloth bathrobe. The white belt accentuated her slim figure which Willis couldn't help but admire.

"Is reading the *Times* something you typically do?" he asked, looking over with interest at the first page of the paper.

"Old habits are hard to break. I've been reading the *Times* ever since I was a teenager, Besides, today it's a good distraction, as I found yesterday to be severely upsetting. Poor Hal. I can't imagine facing his situation. What would you do, Willis, if you were in his shoes?"

Willis thought and was fascinated by her clear sense of concern for Hal. He thought for a moment or two, and then said, "Hard to say. I don't know. If it were me, I guess I would review my life and see if there was any aspect of it that I would want to make, shall we say, 'an adjustment'... Maybe risk a new adventure."

Laura stared at Willis for a long time until she quietly got up and went back into the house without a word. Willis was deeply concerned that he had inadvertently upset her. He consequently did one of his typical assessments of his life, which he tended to do from time to time. While he had always considered his mother and Laura contemporaries, Laura was really more his equal in age than that of his mother. She was what—probably four or so years older than he. If faced with the reality of the situation, he would have to admit that he was more than just casually attracted to her… a rather shocking realization on his part.

He tried to shake that thought, but in spite of his efforts, he had to admit while he was finding her to be complex, he was also finding her more and more desirable! Now that certainly gave him pause. He tried to shake the idea, but the seed had been planted and he wondered if she would tend to him as she did with her beloved bonsai. He soon heard the garage door open and her car pulled out. Willis didn't hear a word from her for the rest of the morning.

Willis kept himself occupied by spending time answering some emails and texts and then putting them aside, he started running down what he had learned about Laura's concerns to date. He also had started to develop a theory about what was going on with the murders and suspicious deaths, and that required some rather deep, systematic thinking on his part. He was soon knee-deep in researching on his computer. Late that morning his cell phone rang, and when he answered, he heard a voice on the other end say, "Inspector Willis?"

"Yes, that's me. Who's calling?" he asked, as he didn't recognize the phone number.

"It's Patty Parker, I work at the lab that tested the sample peach that you left here the other day. Christopher is off for the weekend, but he asked me to call you the second we got the results from that peach."

"And?" asked Willis with considerable concern.

"Well, Inspector if our preliminary results are accurate, that peach looks like it was treated with a chemical called Axicoranate phosphorous, a poison which, once digested, is almost impossible to trace. If our further tests prove this is true, then that piece of fruit had enough poison on it to kill a linebacker... in fact, a whole team! We're curious as to where that poison might have come from, as it's quite unusual. It's occasionally found in some pharmacies as it can be used to kill certain exotic strains of illnesses but should only be used in extremely small doses and under VERY careful supervision because of its obvious dangers. It is rarely used these days, because once it's digested, if it isn't in an extremely small dose, it is almost always lethal and, again, almost impossible to detect. Really, it has not been readily available commercially for a long, long time for obvious reasons. How on earth did it ever get on that peach? Of course, we need to do some additional testing, but it seems obvious to me that whoever put that poison on the peach intended to kill someone."

"Now that's very interesting," replied Willis. "I have no idea as to its source but I certainly intend to find out. Thank you so much for your help, Patty. Please thank Christopher for me."

Willis gently put down his phone, and, rubbing his chin, was deep in thought. *With that information, it certainly looks like there's a killer out there.*

Just then Laura knocked softly on his door and asked, "How about a bite of lunch?" Gone were any signs of any annoyance or disturbance on her part. It was almost as if nothing had transpired earlier that morning. *Very odd,* thought Willis.

Lunch consisted of a platter of cold cuts, cheeses, pickles, and potato salad plus an assortment of breads and rolls that were beautifully arranged and looked delicious. *Really a bit of overkill,* thought Willis, *but very thoughtful.* The food had been set out on plates that Willis recognized as being hand painted from Italy… a festival of blue, white, and yellow. They were identical to the ones his mother had bought when the two ladies had gone off to Italy together years ago. As Laura put the platter down in the center of the breakfast table, she asked, "What would you like to drink? There's green tea, iced tea, water, sodas, or coffee."

Willis thought for the moment, asked, "What are you having?

To which Laura said, "Green tea," and Willis replied, "I'll have the same. Sounds delicious. I'm very partial to tea." Soon there were two tall glasses of tea with ice on the table, each with a sprig of mint.

"There you go… Enjoy!" she said, and they both started to eat quietly, each deep in his and her own thoughts. After a while, Willis said, "Am I crazy but didn't you used to have long hair… you know, down to the middle of your back?"

Laura grinned and finally said, "Well, yes, I had grown it long for years and I really loved the look of it. It was a lot of work, but I could do so many things with it. I had a wonderful hairstylist named Ski who was amazingly talented and also charming... He was an excellent combination as 'getting one's hair cared for' and also kind of having 'a form of therapy session.' Oh, the things I told Ski over the years! One day he was thinning my hair out as it was long and quite truthfully very heavy. Well, he grabbed the wrong scissors and when he went to thin the one side, he cut it off as he had grabbed a regular pair of scissors! It was an unbelievable nightmare!"

"What did you do?' asked Willis

Laura smiled at the memory. "We both looked in the mirror and cried! It was awful. And I have to say in a strange way it cut our trust in each other. I never felt safe with him after that. Yes, I know accidents happen, but this was every woman's nightmare. It was almost like having one's hair fall out… that awful."

"So, what happened? Willis prodded.

"Well, I told him, 'We have two choices here. I can get up and walk out and never come back or you can give me free hair treatments for the rest of the year.' Thank God he was smart and took the latter offer and we've continued our relationship. Best of all, would you believe I kind of grew to like the new look. It's easier to handle, and it gave me a fresh… I don't know… sort of a new way of looking at things. Crazy, eh?"

The two smiled at the idea and returned to eating. After a while, Willis looked up and said, "I had some very disturbing news this morning."

"Oh?" asked Laura.

"I got a call today from a lab I was referred to. Last Friday, when I was over at Claudine's, on impulse, I took a peach from a bowl that was on her kitchen counter and had it analyzed and I got a preliminary report back this morning."

"Oh," said Laura. She tilted her head in surprise.

"Well, the interesting thing is they believe the peach had an unusual poison on it. A poison that was extremely strong. I think there's a distinct possibility that someone put poison on the fruit and Claudine died from it. Of course, I'll need to inform the police of this."

"Oh my God! Who would do such a terrible thing? But

of course, as you know, I've been concerned about such things happening around here. What are you going to do about it?"

"Well, the lab plans to do more studies on it to make absolutely sure that they're correct about the analysis. If turns out that the peach contained that poison, as I'm sure it did, then I'll need to inform the police. It'll prove that your concerns around here are well-founded and certainly a serious concern. I must congratulate you, Laura. It was very astute of you to have suspected that there's a killer on the loose here."

With a sigh, Laura said, "Oh, that's terrible. It will scare everyone around here, not to mention it will be really bad news for Sunningdale and its reputation! Is there any way to delay this so folks like Carl Stone, who runs Sunningdale, can get some control over the situation? It would be really appreciated. Something like this could ruin the place."

"Well, Laura, if it turns out that the lab is 100 percent correct, then I really must inform the police. Meanwhile, I need to go over to her villa right away and secure the fruit so no one else can get hurt from it."

"Oh of course… I just wish there was a way to keep this quiet."

"Unfortunately, I won't be able to if the lab officially confirms what we now suspect."

"Tell me, Willis, what's it like being away from the police force?"

Willis paused for a moment, then said, "It's interesting, Laura. At first, I thought it would be really different being away from all that police structure, for lack of a better term. It turns out that I certainly don't miss all that paperwork, but I do on occasion miss the inner workings of the force that enables one to research and develop theories about crimes as they pop up, bounce ideas off of fellow policemen, and be able to compare theories. However, in truth, I have so much stored up here," he said, pointing to his head, "that I can in certain ways zero in on a subject without much of a problem. I certainly enjoy working with the folks I choose to work with and not be stuck with someone I'm, shall I say, not compatible with. It helps that I have Ross and Monty, my assistants, backing me up. They're so supportive and valuable."

"I would not have been able to come here if I didn't have those two wonderful guys covering for me during the time I'm away. I'd love for you to meet them sometime. They've become almost like sons to me. While they're identical twins, they were raised in totally different environments, which means they often have different ways of looking at things, and often this is very valuable. For example: earlier I called them and was talking about how I enjoyed dinner here the other night. Monty wanted to know what the dinner guests were like, what they did for a living, how they lived and so forth, while Ross was more interested in whether there were any women his age in attendance and, if so, what they were like."

Laura smiled and tried to act as though she understood what he was saying, but it had been a while since she had thought in those terms and, of course, she had never been a parent.

"So, are your 'boys' pushing you to date and possibly get married?" she asked with a hint of a mischievous smile.

"Probably, but they're very subtle and devious, so it's sometimes hard to tell what they're up to. I love my work and up to now that's been enough stimulation for me, but I don't know... Things seem to be changing," he said with a grin.

Laura smiled at this thought and hoped she was reading Willis correctly.

Willis, feeling that perhaps the conversation might be getting a bit too personal, thought maybe he should change the subject. After all, Laura had been very close his mother, and so he felt a bit awkward and ill at ease when it came to intimate talk with this woman who he barely knew but who he was rapidly becoming more and more attracted to.

After a bit of silence, they each took up something to

read, Laura a copy of *Interior Design* and Willis took out his laptop and started reading a subject that dealt with child psychology, not the average person's choice but, nevertheless, a subject that fascinated him.

About ten or fifteen minutes later, Willis looked up and said in a soft voice, "What was your childhood like Laura? Just curious." He wanted to understand her better.

The silence between the two hung like a dense fog that seemingly wouldn't lift until Laura said in a very small voice, "Oh I don't know, I hardly remember my first five years. Not sure why, but it's mostly a blank. Sure, I can tell you that we had a very comfortable life, almost a fairytale type of existence in that my parents were deeply in love with each other and, in turn, showered me with affection. From what I can tell from old photographs, I was a very pretty little girl, always photographed in beautiful clothes, you know, lots of ruffles and bows, but for some reason, I have very few memories from that time. Apparently, something happened around the time I was five. I'm not sure what it was, but I suddenly was unable to speak. I don't know. Who knows what goes on in a little girl's mind? My parents were frantic and took me to see all sorts of doctors. The doctors thought that maybe something had traumatized me. I don't know."

"What I do remember of that period of time was, I had

an uncle, Uncle Conrad, my mother's brother, who was quite close to us. Well, one day he went out with my dad fishing and... I'm not sure of the details but it seems the canoe they were in tipped over and Uncle Conrad couldn't swim and he drowned. My father was an excellent swimmer and so survived, but he was unable to save Uncle Conrad. It was awful and my father refused to ever discuss it even years later. My mother, I think, blamed my dad and their relationship was strained for a long period after that. Around that time, I slowly regained my voice, but we never knew what had caused my loss in the first place."

Laura had been looking at her feet the whole time and finally looked up and there were tears in her eyes. She quickly brushed them away along with the memories of that time, got up, went to the kitchen, and called back to Willis, "Want some coffee? If so, I'll make a pot." And that was that. Willis had the feeling that he might never get Laura to say more about the subject.

Later that day, Willis on impulse asked Laura, "Would you please give me Else Carning's phone number?"

"Sure, but why on earth would you want that?"

"Oh, I don't know... just a hunch. From what little I've seen of her, I'm fascinated by her and I think she might be insightful about the goings on here at Sunningdale."

"Good luck with her. Else can be a bit of a prima donna. I'm afraid in the process of building her huge career, and it was HUGE, she created an ego on an equal scale. In all the time I've known her, she has never appeared in the same outfit… not once! Nor has she ever changed her mind… on ANYTHING! She tends to take a stand on everything and then never ever changes her opinion on things."

Now this I have to see, mused Willis. He took down Else's number and called her later when Laura was out of the room. He wasn't sure exactly why he was being secretive about Else with Laura, but instinct told him to keep any forthcoming information and thoughts close to his chest.

When Willis dialed Else's number, he got a very terse phone message. It simply said, "Leave a number!" That was it. No "Hello, this is Else", or even a "Hi, please leave a message."

So Willis said, "Hi, this is Willis. We met last night at Shelia's. I found you very interesting and I've been lamenting the fact that we didn't get to talk more. I'd love to get together with you over coffee or a drink at some point so I can get to know you a bit better." He then added his cell number so that Else could reply if and when she wanted to.

With that done, he went into the kitchen in search of some more coffee, as somehow Laura's earlier offer of coffee never materialized. Searching around the kitchen, he promptly found on the sideboard one of those small coffee makers that had a selection of various coffee blends in small cups that, in theory, one could put into the coffeemaker and magically have a wonderful cup of coffee. Why she had two different coffee makers was a puzzle to Willis. *Sometimes*, he thought, *it was like she was of two minds.*

The only problem was the darn coffee maker didn't work! Obviously, he was missing a step or two to get the machine to produce that special cup of coffee. *When will mankind stop making things more difficult than necessary?* he mused. He was about to tackle the other coffee maker when his thoughts were interrupted by the sound of his cell ringing. When he looked at it, it was a call coming in that looked vaguely familiar as it should have been, as it was Else on the other end of the line when they got connected.

"Yes?" said Willis.

"Willis, is that you? I believe you called me," said the voice with that slight Danish accent.

"Oh, hi, Else. Thanks for returning my call. I so enjoyed the brief time we had together last night. Would you be interested in having a cup of coffee or a drink sometime?" Willis couldn't help thinking, *Well, that would be one way to get a cup of coffee!*

"Oh, that would be delightful," replied Else. "When

were you thinking of getting together and where?"

"Well, if it would work for you, how about meeting at that small coffee shop near the gym here in Sunningdale sometime this afternoon?"

"Oh, why not drop by my place? I'm in the tower. Number 1805… the 18th floor. I'll be free in about a half hour or so. Would that work for you?"

"Perfect," replied Willis. "I'll see you then." And they both hung up.

Willis went in search of Laura and found her once again reading the *New York Times*. This time she was out in her back yard on a lounge chair. When he found her, he said, "Isn't that sun a bit too much for you? If you'd like, I can move that umbrella over here and give you a little protection."

"Oh, don't bother. In the later years of my life, I've taken to wearing lots of sunscreen. You should, too."

"Well, I'm naturally dark, so it's been less of a problem for me than for most folks," he replied, "but thanks for your concern." However, he recalled the warning that Tony had given him. *Hmmm, timing*, he thought. A little later he announced, "By the way, I'm going out for a bit but I should be back in an hour or two."

"Oh, where are you off to, Willis?"

"Nowhere in particular," he replied, and out he went

wondering why he had been so evasive. He walked over to the Tower, which was a short, pleasant walk as the day had turned out to be extremely comfortable with lots of sun and a mild, gentle breeze. The Tower was surrounded by a border of tall palm trees that obviously had been there for quite a long time—*or maybe not*— thought Willis. So much of the landscaping had a Disney-like quality in that a huge effort appeared to have been made to have everything look perfect. Every palm was as close to being identical to its neighboring tree, and so there was a kind of unreal look to the place. Willis later learned that during a recent hurricane, many of the palm trees had been destroyed, but the people running Sunningdale had quickly had the damaged palms replaced with full-grown palms so the image of perfection would be maintained.

Willis walked up the sidewalk and entered the Tower's lobby, which was impressive in scale and decor. The entry consisted of lots of light tan flooring and walls painted to match. The light coming through the large windows offered a view of a pond, which was a bit smaller than the one that the villas encircled, but was equally handsome. It had its own fountain, which Willis later learned was never turned off. At night it was lit by pale blue lights which were hidden under the water.

As Willis entered the lobby, he spotted a reception desk

and nearby was a sign directing people to the video center and the auditorium. There was a selection of medium-sized video screens announcing current and future events that would be in the offing, including a concert by Cyndi Lauper. *Hmmm*, thought Willis, *that's an interesting choice for an older crowd, but then...*

Willis promptly found the elevators and pushed the "up" button. After quite a wait, an elevator arrived. He entered it, pushed the button labeled eighteen, and was quietly taken to that level. As the door opened, Willis was deposited into what he was later to learn was the colony lounge, which was about 40 feet by 40 feet and had a ceiling that was a good 25 feet above the carpeted floor. The furniture was high-end and there was a huge, strikingly handsome modern painting on the wall opposite the elevator bank. Here and there were pieces of modern sculpture. Clearly, the people who lived in this colony were very well-off and sophisticated.

Willis was to later find out that Else was the main force in choosing the decor for this colony's lounge area; however, some of the people in the colony had put up some pieces of their own art collections, much to Else's chagrin. She was currently on a very active campaign to change out their art for pieces which Else thought were more desirable. It promised to become an interesting debate.

Willis checked the apartment numbers and soon found

Else's apartment door. Next to it was a simple pedestal with a very handsome piece of sculpture that Willis was later to learn was by an up-and-coming sculptor, Nando Kallweit. There was also a fascinating painting by Maria Esmar in a colorful and harmonious composition.

Willis rang the doorbell and the door immediately opened to reveal Else in an outfit that looked like it had come straight out of *Vogue* magazine. It was a rather unusual rust red with a matching rust and white scarf that echoed the same red as the rest of her outfit. While Else's hands betrayed the falsehood of the age she claimed to be, the rest of her appeared to be a testament to the skills of several plastic surgeons—or so the word was. Added to her natural elegance and superb taste in clothing was the fact that she had impeccable posture. In short, she looked terrific!

Word was that she always wore extremely handsome outfits and every selection in her wardrobe was theatrical and stunning. Apparently, at one point in her career, she was a bit of a renegade in that she had pockets added to all her outfits. She was quoted as saying, "I'll be damned if I'll lug a purse around which is easier to steal. I prefer a pocket to a bag!"

As the door swung open, she said, "Ah, welcome to my home," as she gestured with a rather grand sweep of her hand for Willis to enter. Willis found it curious that while

Else put forth a broad grin, pleasure somehow didn't reach her eyes.

I wonder what that's about? he mused.

"Thanks for coming over, Inspector. I'm so glad to have a chance for a one-on-one get-together with you." Again, there was that smile but again without any real warmth.

"Well, Else, we never really got to talk the other night so I'm glad to have this opportunity to get to know you a bit better." This time there was a hint of warmth in her look. "Tell me, have you been a resident here for long and what brought you here?"

"It was my husband, Patrick, who prompted the move here. He had been having, how should I say it, the promise of some health issues, as his twin brother had already come down with the early stages of Alzheimer's, and while Carl hadn't had any major health problems, we thought we would be wise to move in so, should the need arise, we'd be in a safe, supportive environment. It proved to be a smart move, as half a year after we moved in, Carl started to have some minor health issues. I have to say, the staff here is remarkably helpful and supportive when the chips are down, as you Americans say. Now enough of that. Please have a seat."

She gestured towards a large, elegant chair which had a three-inch chrome band wrapped around the sides and back of the chair, which made the chair not only beautiful but unique. It also turned out to be very comfortable.

"Ah", said Willis. "You clearly have an accent. Are you Swedish?"

"Oh no, I'm 100 percent Danish," she said with a big smile.

"How did you end up here, since you appear to be rather proud of your mother country?"

"Curious question, as you Americans seldom take the time to ask. I was born in a small town named Faaborg. While we weren't rich in kroner, we were rich in education and ambition. Our one claim to fame was that my family had a piano… the only one in town. We also had a rather extensive library, including a great many books that dealt with decorating."

"Interesting," said Willis.

"Well, yes, I found decorating to be both exciting and stimulating, and so I studied it and soon realized that if I were to reach any heights in the field, I would have to devote myself to my craft. I studied hard and worked with some of the top designers of my day. I know it doesn't sound very modest, but I became very good at my craft. I moved here to the States, as that was where all the action was. Come, Willis, take a look around this apartment and you'll see what I mean. I think you'll find that there is no apartment in Sunningdale as elegant and handsome as this one. I call it 'My Sarasota Loft.'"

Willis thought, *Hmmm, original, and some ego!*

She gestured for him to follow her through the living room. "You probably haven't seen many of the apartments here in Sunningdale, but let me tell you'll never see one as beautifully designed as this one."

While Willis marveled at her lack of modesty, he looked around and saw what she was talking about. While the apartment wasn't overly large, it gave the impression of being quite spacious. The floors were covered in rich white tiles, occasionally broken up with carpets in soft beiges and grays. The walls were mostly a similar white with a hint of gray here and there, with full-length mirrors that extended the look of the various rooms.

The living room featured a fireplace that was simply a horizontal opening maybe a foot and a half high by probably four feet in length. While an open flame of any type, including candles, was strictly forbidden in Sunningdale, the flames in this fireplace looked absolutely real. Else explained that they were, in fact, vapor flickering flames... very real looking but safe. One could actually put one's hands through the flame without getting burnt!

Throughout the apartment there were extraordinarily handsome antiques and a few tapestries, some exquisite rugs, a few sculptures, and some fine oil paintings. Willis noted that they were labeled, some having been painted as far back as the late 1500s, including a Lucas Cranach painting of Adam and Eve. These paintings and the few antique pieces of furniture shone as they stood out against all the surrounding soft modern textures and colors. The furniture, like the first chair Willis saw, was elegantly simple and modern, mostly in whites and pale grays that accentuated the handsome simplicity of the rooms and made the antiques the stars of the rooms. Not that there were different rooms, as the design was such that the dining area led into the living room, and that, in turn, led on to the master bedroom.

The apartment was all one flowing space with the kitchen framing one end of the apartment with its pale gray cabinets topped by a very large white stone countertop with some gray veining that streamed throughout it.

The backsplash had a flowing light gray pattern which provided an attractive background without screaming for attention. All of the hardware was a brushed silver, very sleek, very handsome. Perhaps the most stunning part of the place was the bank of floor-to-ceiling windows that totally filled one side of the apartment. It must have been 50 or 55 feet long and ended with an outside, covered terrace beyond. The windows and terrace all overlooked a stunning view of the bay below.

The bedroom was currently in full view at the other end

of the living space with its simple, modern canopied bed. It had a pristine white bedspread and headboard flanked with handsome nightstands with brushed chrome light fixtures above them. Else referred to it as her "loft" and at one point pushed a button and demonstrated that a wall that was mirrored floor to ceiling could move out of a hidden pocket in the wall and close off the bedroom if desired. Because this wall was fully mirrored, it echoed the rest of the living room and dining room and maintained the large airy feeling of the apartment.

Else then showed Willis the master bathroom and the huge walk-in closet with its shelves for 50 or so shoes, not to mention the long rows of hanging spaces for her numerous outfits. She went on to show him the guestroom and its bathroom plus an office which, while very small, was designed to be very efficient and had sliding doors that could open up onto the terrace. When the tour was over, it became obvious that while Else was certainly not modest, she clearly knew her business and was extremely talented.

Willis smiled and announced, "Your place is amazing. I've never quite seen such a handsome space before. You certainly did a wonderful job. There's no question that you're a master of your profession, Else." Willis's compliment was two-fold. First, he really meant it, but also he had long ago found that giving someone a compliment often loosened up that person... made them more assessable. In truth, her "loft" was original, but certainly would not suit the tastes of most people who lived in Sunningdale.

She glowed with this compliment and, making a wide sweeping gesture with her hands, said, "Well, it's wonderful that you like it, Willis. It took a great deal of care and attention to get these results and I can tell you, it was worth it. I clearly know how to decorate, having won many awards over the years, and while I know that this place is special, it's always nice to hear a compliment now and then."

Willis thought, *Else is an interesting combination of talent and ego.* Else interrupted his thought with, "Now, shall we have some tea or would you prefer something stronger?"

"Tea would be perfect, thank you, as I'm particularly partial to that brew."

Soon they were sitting on the large pale gray sofa that had very clean, super smooth lines and had a coffee table which held a small variety of foods arranged artfully on a handsome tray that looked like it might have been made from a hammered metal of some sort.

"So, Willis, what have you found out so far about Claudine Hollar's death? Was she in fact murdered?" It was a question that he hadn't expected and if he had, he would have thought she might have been more subtle. Clearly, she was a direct person who had asked a direct question and, as such, deserved a direct answer.

"Hmmm," said Willis. He picked up a small sandwich-like creation, rubbed his chin a bit, and then took a bite as a stalling device before saying, "If you're referring to Claudine's unusual death, then I have to say there's a lot there that doesn't meet one's eye, at least on the surface. While initially it looked like a suicide what with the pills found on her body, that's not the full story. I can't go into details, but I can tell you in all probability her death was no suicide."

"Hmmm, I wondered," she said with a slight air of satisfaction on her face.

"Now why would you think that?"

"Well for starters, she wasn't very likable."

"How so?"

"Well, she was rather snobbish… into *being* part of a clique that excluded others."

"What do you mean by that?" he asked.

"Well, she had a rather wicked way of snubbing others… she really, in some ways, deserved to have someone get back at her, get even with her. Let me explain." Else straightened her posture as if she were arming herself to project a sense of strength and rigidity that would make her comments stronger… more important.

"After seeing my apartment, she approached me to help

decorate her place. We had several meetings and I worked hard on developing some ideas for her, but she really was a piece of work. Ultimately, she had lots of bad design ideas and not the good sense to use my ideas, which were really quite wonderful."

Hmmm, thought Willis. *Now that's interesting. Actually, Else should talk about being snobbish.* Willis thought for a while about the ramifications if someone were to reject Else's design ideas. He first decided to ask some generalized questions of her with the hopes that the answers might shed some light on what was generally going on in Sunningdale, and what specifically had happened to Claudine.

So, he decided to ask her some leading questions. "Tell me, Else, you said that you were born in Denmark. How did you end up here in the States?"

"Well, as I mentioned, I was born in Denmark and actually spent the first 25 years of my life there, but I had an older brother who had immigrated to the States and who was, I think, a bit homesick, so rather than return to Denmark, he had the brilliant idea of bringing Denmark to the States. His plan was to have all five of his siblings come over to New York City where he lived. Well, it worked for me, but the others weren't as adventurous or up for such a move."

"I, as it turned out, jumped at the chance to live a new and different life, and so I moved to New York. To everyone's surprise, I thrived on the City and all it had to offer, and I soon was taking courses in English and continued my studies in interior decorating. The latter became a passion for me. Luckily the style of 'Danish Modern' came into vogue around that time, and I was a natural for selling it to designers. After meeting many of them, I decided that I could do a better job at decorating other people's homes and offices than they did."

"In short, I had found my niche. I was not only a natural at designing, I was also a very good salesperson and that's what interior designers really are. Sure, they have to come up with good design ideas, but they also have to pitch them. And so, I developed a very enjoyable and lucrative career. I'm one of those people who tends to look forward but has a solid appreciation of things past. That's why this apartment is so successful, in that it's a forward-looking environment that also has an appreciation of the past."

She paused and Willis had the feeling that a compliment might be in order and might, in fact, bring out some more information from her. So he said, "I'm fascinated by the fact that you always seem to be wearing something different every time I see you which, granted, hasn't been that often, but I hear that you never repeat any of your outfits. Is that true?

Else smiled and said, "Of course it's not totally true but

I seldom repeat outfits. I try to vary them a great deal. It's kind of a fun game of mine, no, make that a passion. Luckily, I have a fantastic dressmaker and I can show her a photo of an outfit I like and have her make a copy of it. Often, I request that she make a slight change in one of my outfits which I have worn in the past, such as add a sash or a scarf for color, whatever, and voila! A new outfit. You know a scarf can add a lot of drama and color to an outfit. Other outfits are ones that I've picked up in my many travels. For example, that floor-length blue and white outfit I wore the other day was something I picked up in the small shop in Marrakesh. Wasn't the embroidery on it amazing?"

Willis smiled as he enjoyed the ingenuity of this woman. However, he was bothered by the dark gray dress she currently had on as it reminded him of the outfit that was worn by the person he saw brushing what he now knew was poison on the peaches in the back of Claudine's yard. Maybe this is just a coincidence he thought...but maybe not!

Willis mulled this over and while he felt Else was a bit of an egotist and most likely an opportunist, she was also clearly very talented and clever. He was not so sure how she would react if someone tried to cross her, as he remembered overhearing her say the other day when he first met her, "I don't tolerate people who cross me.... I get even!"

I'd hate to ever get on the wrong side of her! he thought.

So, after an enjoyable and fascinating time with her, Willis excused himself and got up to leave when Else threw in a thought as he headed for the door.

Smiling, she said, "Have you by chance had a chance to talk to Matty? I don't mean in a causal way but deeply. She's a very smart, observant lady and might help you with your investigation, if that's what you're calling your activities around here." Willis looked at her with a bit of surprise on his face. "Of course, we all know what you're up to," she said with a little pat on his shoulder as she opened the door for him to make his exit.

Lots for me to think about. Maybe I should try to corner Matty and see what she might have to say about all that's going on.

He returned to Laura's to find her greatly agitated ,but when he asked her what was wrong, she either chose to not discuss it or couldn't. She just seemed to be really preoccupied. Thinking that maybe he should give her some more time to herself, Willis announced, "I think I'll give you some space and go for a walk.

"Whatever," she said, almost absentmindedly as she went to the other side of the house.

He quietly let himself out and headed around the lake

with the thought of wandering by Matty's place, but in the process, he stumbled onto Bruton, who was sitting on his usual bench.

On a whim, he asked, "Mind if I join you?"

"Nope, help yourself," was Bruton's reply as he shifted over to one end of the bench and gestured for Willis to join him. This time the birds with the bright red plumage were nowhere in sight, much to Willis's disappointment.

"Where are your buddies with the bright red plumage?" Willis asked.

"Oh, they're like good weather... Here some days and gone the next, similar to the folk around here. How's your inspection coming along... It is 'Inspector Willis', is it not?"

Willis opted to not bother to request that Bruton not use the word "Inspector", as it just wasn't worth the effort, and, in truth, wasn't all that important and so he just nodded. They sat there for a while not talking, just mostly enjoying watching the birds.

Finally, Bruton said, "Any progress in finding out what's going on around here?" Willis decided to play dumb and act like he didn't know what "going on around here" meant.

When Willis was not forthcoming with any information, Bruton said, "Do you know if Claudine was murdered like the rumor has it? We certainly aren't hearing anything from the folks who run this place or the police!" With that, he took a swig from his water bottle.

Willis countered by saying, "That's what we're trying to find out. What's your take on all this?"

"Hmmm." Bruton said. "Well, it's not as if Claudine would win any popularity contest around here. She, in fact, really annoyed a great number of the folks here but I don't know... why would anyone go so far as to want to kill her?" He paused as if deep in thought and then said, "No, I think she must have taken those pills they found by her body. Someone said the other day that this wasn't the first time she tried to kill herself. Word has it that she took an overdose a long time ago but someone found her before it wasn't too late and called 911. Not sure how true that is, but it's kinda interesting."

Willis nodded his head as if he concurred, but then said, "Why do you suppose she could have killed herself?" He wondered if Bruton might just be playing dumb himself, and might, in fact, know more than he was letting on… or was he, most probably, just a harmless gossip.

In any case, he simply shrugged in reply to Willis's question. When there was no real response from Bruton, Willis said, to change the subject, "I had a nice talk with Tony the other day. How well do you know him?"

"Oh, just so-so. He certainly presents himself as one of the outstanding members of the community here. He's constantly mentioning that he's 96, which gets to be a bit much after a while, but I guess it's a badge of honor of sorts. Too bad he was forced to leave his practice, but my guess is he probably didn't mention that."

"No, can't say that he did. What happened?"

"Of course, it's all hearsay," Bruton said, acting very serious and very dramatic. "But the word is he had a terrible accident that was job-related. He had a patient die which, of course, is not all that unusual for a doctor who specialized in geriatrics, but apparently it was totally Tony's fault..." And Bruton sat there and didn't go any further.

After a long pause, he said, "Yup, everyone around here has a story. It's an odd collection of people around here. I, for one, am probably not a good source for any investigating that you're doing around here, as I don't necessarily get along with most of the occupants and, therefore, don't really interact with them. I know, they all appear to be quite friendly, but believe me, it's a veneer. You'd be surprised at how conniving and self-serving many of the folks around here are. Can't say I really like many of them. No, these are my friends." He gestured towards the birds he had been feeding.

After a long pause, Willis turned to Bruton and asked, "Are you married?"

There was a long pause and Bruton finally replied, "Yes and no."

"How so?

"Well, my wife left me four years ago."

"Oh, I'm sorry to hear it. How did you cope with that?" asked Willis.

After a long pause where Bruton took a drink from his water bottle, he replied, "No, it's not what you're thinking. Four years ago, Carla developed dementia. It started with her repeating stories over and over again. She simply seemed to forget that she had just told that particular story. Well, her memory soon left her and she ended up in Sunningdale's Memory Care unit. I used to visit her often, but most times she just didn't recognize me, even when I would show her photos of our life together. It was disturbing at first, but then I just accepted her condition and made sure she was well taken care of. It was all so strange."

"She used to play solitaire for hours, but finally she didn't even do that. It's sad to say it, but she was gone before she was gone. One day after I had spent a lot of time with her, helping to feed her and so forth, I left and soon after I got home, I got a call saying that she had passed away. Just like that. Gone... and, sad to say, it was a relief for me."

"I'm so sorry. What was the cause, if you don't mind my asking?"

"Oh, I don't know. She had been fading for so long... I guess they all felt it was just a matter of time and then her time was up."

Willis put his arm around Bruton to comfort him, but he thought, *I wonder if he helped her die. Sometimes when a partner feels the other one is totally mentally gone, the partner finds a way to help the sick one to "leave".*

Willis sensed that there was more, so he said, "Please, go on."

"Well, it's not my only loss. I had a younger brother named R.K. who I was very close to. God, he was a golden man. Perfect... a great athlete, smart as all-get-out and oh, I just adored him. We were very close. He was very active in the community. You know, a Boy Scout leader, a volunteer fireman, the works. Well one day the fire alarm sounded, and the volunteer firemen all ran down to the firehouse and everyone hopped onto the fire truck as it started to tear off to the fire or whatever was the emergency. Well, R.K. was one of the last guys to arrive and as he reached the truck, he slipped on some oil on the floor and fell and slid under the truck just as it pulled out and it ran over him!"

"It was awful…very upsetting to all the men in the fire department, but to me it was a devastating loss. He was my best friend. I never really got over it. In a way I've never trusted… never had a close friend after that. So now I have my birds," he said, gesturing towards the pond.

"It's been—what, two or so years now since Carla died…

I'm a bit of a loner, not much for socializing. I wonder if I'd like to have some human company in my life." There was a long pause, then he blurted out, "Do you think Laura might consider..." But he failed to finish the thought.

After a long pause, Willis said, "Oh look, our friends with the red plumage just flew in. Aren't they beautiful?" and Bruton nodded. There was another long pause, and then Bruton suddenly said, "Damn, there's that fucking swan again. You know, swans mate for life and that one lost his mate a while ago and he's become meaner by the day." Bruton pointed towards the single swan that was aggressively swimming past the birds with the red plumage and pecking at one of them which got in his way.

"I'm going to get rid of that fucker!"

Willis looked at him in surprise, as Bruton was getting red with rage. "How would you ever do that?" Willis asked.

"Oh, that'll be easy. I'll just look up poisons on the internet. I'll find one, order it online and when it comes I'll put it on some bread and then that greedy, mean sonofabitch will join his dead mate!" There was a bit of a pause and he muttered under his breath, "I'll get you, just you wait!"

He was quiet for a while, took a drink from his water bottle and when he finally calmed down, he announced rather grandly, "Well, it's past the birds' feeding time. I'd best get them their dinner."

And so, they parted and Willis took out his cell phone along with a list of names and numbers he had put together and was carrying in his pocket. He looked up Matty's number and called her.

Luckily, she answered the call on the third ring with a short, curt "Hello?".

Willis quickly said, "Hi, Matty, I've been meaning to track you down and have a little chat with you. Would you be agreeable to that?"

There was a slight pause which had Willis a little concerned, but ultimately, she replied, "Sure, actually I've been meaning to suggest we have a 'chat' as you call it."

Willis responded, "I'm having a walk around the pond by the villas and can meet you wherever is good for you."

"Oh, your timing is perfect. I just came back from getting something cleared up with my computer at the Computer Center here in the building. Why don't you come over to my place? I'm on the 10th floor, T1007."

"Perfect, I'll be right over," and he headed down the path towards the Tower. As in the past, there was a considerable wait for one of the elevators to arrive, but once Willis was in it and he pushed the button for the 10th floor, it whisked him up smoothly to the desired floor with barely a sound. Like Else's floor, the elevator opened to a large common room for the residents of that floor. Willis found this room to be warmer, more user-friendly, but not nearly as chic as the one on Else's floor.

Willis, after one false move which took him in the wrong direction, was able to easily find his way to #1007 and, after ringing the doorbell, Matty opened the door and greeted Willis with a warm welcoming smile. *Quite a difference from Else's greeting*, thought Willis. "Thank you so much for seeing me on such short notice," he said. Once again, she appeared in an outfit that was seemingly just thrown haphazardly together without any attempt of coordinating the colors or style.

Hmmm, he thought, *it's not every day that one sees orange and green slacks mixed with a pink blouse and that same damned ugly brown sweater that she wore the night before.*

"Actually, I've been meaning to track you down, as I've been mulling over some thoughts which I've wanted to bounce off you, if you don't mind," she said.

"Mind? I'm all ears."

"Please have a chair over here," she said as she pointed at a sitting area that had a collection of five mismatched chairs. "I'd offer you something to drink, but I'm afraid all I have is water as I am not much an 'entertainer of guests'-type person. It's rare that I ever have anyone over here." With that, the two of them sat down.

Willis smiled and said, "Thanks for the offer but it's

not necessary." He said this to initially reassure her that he didn't expect to be offered anything, but also to pave the way for her to be comfortable enough to open up if she had anything important to divulge. To kind of get things rolling, he asked, "How long have you been a resident here at Sunningdale?"

"Hmmm, maybe six years or so. I came here because I have no family to fall back on, not that I would if I could. It's interesting, I've seen so many people who've waited too long to decide to have a backup plan and when it finally dawns on them, say maybe after a stroke or heart attack, that they need a place like this, they usually face a long wait to get an apartment here, if they in fact can pass the physical exam and financially qualify to get a place here, and it's not cheap."

"Sunningdale is pretty rigid when it comes to letting people move in here. I know folks who have waited a number of years before applying for a place here and then couldn't pass the physical to get in. No, sir. I wasn't going to get caught in a situation like that! What I did was I put myself on the waiting list, and eventually got what is called a 'Starter Unit,' which generally is a very small efficiency unit that, believe me, wasn't a place you'd want to end up in to see you through your last days."

"However, getting a 'Starter Unit' puts you on a special

'inside' list for a bigger, better unit, like my apartment here, which has a nice size living room, as you can see, plus an efficient kitchen, a dining area, and a bedroom and den… All very comfortable. There are larger places for sure, but they're much more expensive and, to be honest, more room than I, as a single person, need. Well, I've kind of spouted off haven't I? Sorry about that." She placed both hands firmly on her knees and said, "Now what can I do for you?"

"I tell you what, Matty, it was clear to me the other night when we spent some time together, that you're smart and very observant. I'm here to find out who killed Claudine, as there is little doubt that she was deliberately poisoned. I'm also very interested in checking out Roz's death, as I don't believe, from what I've learned so far, that her death was an accident."

"I'm convinced there's a common thread here, and I wouldn't be surprised if I might find some other suspicious deaths that have occurred here recently. I'm hoping you might give me a clue or two that might help me solve what's going on here. Tell me, other than Rosaline O'Connor and Claudine Hollar, have there been any other mysterious deaths in the past year or two, and, if so, who do you think might be the killer?"

Matty paused and scratched her rather untidy head. "Well, that's a loaded question," she finally replied. "I've actually thought about this for some time now, but of course no one wants to believe that there could be a killer on the loose here at Sunningdale as life here is SOOO PERFECT," she said with more than a hint of sarcasm. "Well, I'm not so sure. In a way your arrival here has validated my suspicions."

After a pause, Willis said, "So, you think that there could be more than the two victims here as a result of a killer being on the loose here in Sunningdale?"

"Oh, without a doubt, and to be perfectly honest, it scares the hell out of me."

Willis and Matty sat staring at each other, both at a loss for words as their conversation just confirmed their common concern. The question was of course: could he or she be caught before anyone else gets killed?

Willis took a deep breath and said, "Do you have anyone you suspect who might be the killer?"

Matty thought for a moment and finally said, "You say Claudine was definitely poisoned."

Willis nodded his head and said, "No, I didn't actually put that into words but I'm afraid so."

"Hmmm," said Matty. "Rumor has it that she was poisoned, and it was by some exotic poison that's rare and difficult to come by. Is that true?"

Willis nodded his head in agreement.

"I have no idea if there's a connection, but Felicia's husband, Carl, was the head of a good-sized pharmaceutical house. He passed away several years ago, but he used to regale us with all sorts of stories about what drugs could and could not do. He even had a large red book with a breakdown of most drugs that were on the market and available… that is, up until he passed away several years ago. I wonder if Felicia still has that book. It's just a thought," she said with a concerned look on her face.

Willis wondered if the look on Matty's face was a put-on or not.

"Yes, but even if she still had the book and could look up a deadly medicine, how would she get it?"

"Oh, I bet the company is fairly lax about supplying such things, especially to stockholders, and my understanding is she holds a considerable amount of stock in the company. I remember it used to drive Carl crazy about how lax the company was in providing drugs to people who were connected to the company at a certain level. He used to carry on about what a dangerous policy that was. Hard to imagine. Not that I think it would actually happen, but I bet if Felicia wanted a certain drug, all she'd have to do is call someone she knew from earlier times and just ask for it... No questions asked, for sure."

"I thought you and Felicia were close friends. What you're intimating is that she could be the killer."

The two sat staring at each other trying to absorb this new concept. Willis pursed his lips and stroked his chin while deep in thought.

Matty looked Willis straight in the eye and said, "Actually, while she's pleasant enough, in my book she's more looks than brains. She can at times be sharp, but really only with her tongue. But that's a whole other story for another time."

"Is there anyone else you think might be a killer amongst the folks here in Sunningdale?"

There was a long pause while Matty thought, and it turned out that she actually suspected someone, but her hesitancy was due to the need to formulate her suspicion in a manner that had validity and clarity. And so, after a pause she said, "Have you considered Else?"

"Well, of course, I've looked at everyone I've encountered, but I'm curious why Else?"

"For starters, of everyone here in Sunningdale, you probably won't find anyone with a larger ego, and with that ego comes an intolerance towards anyone who does not agree with—or at the very least pretend to agree with—the person in question. Else has very little tolerance for most people. I don't know why, but it just seems to be her nature. You've probably heard her famous comment about people she doesn't like or approve of and that's, and I quote: 'I don't tolerate people who cross me... I get even!'"

Matty went on. "It seems to me that someone as smart as Else, who is by the way as smallminded towards many people as I've ever seen and who has a reputation for speaking her mind so she gets her way, might just do anything to anyone who crossed her." She paused, then said, "By the way, I'm not sure you're aware but she had a real intolerance towards Tony."

"Hmmm, a lot of food for thought, mused Willis. "Anyone else?"

Matty walked over to a nearby window, looked out as if deep in thought, and finally turned around abruptly and facing Willis said, "Hal... Hal North."

"Why would you single him out, Matty?"

"I know it seems wild but I wonder, he's facing what amounts to a death threat. I've heard from various friends that he's deeply depressed these days. It turns out he needs a shoulder replacement on top of everything else, and he's angry and, as I said, depressed and has been striking out at his friends. It's like he's a different person... Unpredictable and maybe a bit dangerous."

Willis looked at his watch and said, "Hmmm, sorry, it's later than I thought. I'd best be getting back to Laura's as I'm sure she's expecting me. Thanks for sharing, Matty, and thanks for your time and insight. Please don't mention any of our conversation to anyone. I want to see where it takes us."

Willis shook Matty's hand and let himself out as Matty just stood there. This conversation had filled her with a scary sense of apprehension. Maybe if Else got wind of what she had just discussed with Willis, it's possible Matty could be the next victim, a new and disturbing feeling for her.

Willis quickly returned to Laura's bungalow and, since he now had a door key, he let himself in and called out, "Hi there, I'm back," out of courtesy.

Laura replied, "I'm here in the study."

Willis said, "I'll be there in a minute. I need to charge my phone." When he got to his room, he thought that he heard the back door bang shut as if slammed by someone very angry. He waited a moment and then walked into the study to find Laura at her desk. It was the one room he really hadn't been into up to now. It was smallish in size and very efficiently set up with a handsome feminine desk, very neat with a small vase with a yellow flower on it. It had, as a companion, a desk chair covered in a delicate yellow patterned print. Next to it was a large chair covered in a strong, almost harsh plaid in red-orange and black, quite the contrast to the desk chair. There were also lots of books neatly arranged in several bookcases. *Hmmm*, thought Willis, *What an interesting room, nice but rather sober in places. I hope I can get a chance to look over the books she has here. I'll be interested to see what she reads. I wonder if part of this room was used by her late husband.*

Laura was quietly writing in what looked like her journal.

Willis asked, "I hope I'm not interrupting you?"

Laura replied without looking up, "Not at all, Willis. I'm almost finished. Please sit down and make yourself comfortable," as she gestured with a nod of her head towards the armchair. "Or get yourself something to drink. By now you know where everything's kept."

Willis took the opportunity to take a look at the various books and found that one shelf contained books on gardening, home decorating, and poetry. The other was dedicated to a totally different selection of works. That one held books devoted to sports, politics, and war. The bookcases were so interesting, so different, so informative.

Moments later she quietly closed the journal, put it away in the base of a grandfather clock in the corner, which Willis noted made for an excellent hiding place as one would never think to look there. It was almost like she was showing Willis where to look should he ever want to read her journal. *Odd*, he thought, but she soon closed her pen (she had been writing with a fountain pen, something else unusual) and turned around to face him.

Another unique thing about this woman, he thought. *When was the last time I saw someone use a fountain pen? Hell, most kids these days can't write or even read script. The world sure keeps changing!*

Noting Willis's fascination with her pen, Laura said, "I'm very partial to using a fountain pen. I know it's passé, but I love the look and feel of it. I keep that journal as it helps to clear my thoughts… at least that's what I tell myself, but I don't know, this murder business has me confused and frightened. I wish you could help me sort things out."

Willis wanted to help her, but was currently at a loss as to how to unravel the mysteries that seemed to swim around her and Sunningdale. Willis went on to say, "I notice that the gray outfit that was hanging in the closet in my room is gone."

"Oh, that old thing, it belongs to a friend of mine who left it here on her last visit. I just remembered it this morning and thought I ought to put it away so you have more room. I hope it wasn't a nuisance."

"Not to worry. It wasn't in the way at all," he said. He tried always to be an easy guest. Then on impulse, he decided to offer to take her out for dinner. "Would you like to go out for dinner? My treat this time... no discussion," he said firmly. While she initially said, "No", with some gentle urging on Willis's part, he was successful in changing her mind by saying, "You seem stressed and my guess is that you could use a change of scenery." They finally agreed that they would walk over to St Armand's Circle, a nearby part of town which was an easy 15-minute walk and where there was a wide selection of restaurants to choose from.

The walk was quite pleasant, as the weather was on the balmy side and people appeared to be in a celebratory mood. Where the previous days had threatened to turn stormy, today it had done a total about face and had been glorious, with nothing but blue, clear skies—a real treat!

They walked together and eventually ended up arm in arm, partially because Willis by nature tended to take long strides and by holding on to Laura, he subconsciously took shorter steps. He also, to his delight, enjoyed the body contact. They arrived in the heart of the little village and faced the need to decide which type of food they wanted, but then discovered that it being a Saturday night, most of the restaurants were very busy with some folks waiting outside for a table to free up.

Several of the restaurants had musicians playing outside for the people who were eating out of doors. One had a guitar player, and one even had a rather good pianist who was using a small beat-up piano that most likely had been rolled out from the inside of the restaurant.

They finally found a small place that had a free, quiet

table, and when they asked the young man who appeared to be in charge if the table was free, they were told to "Help yourselves" as he gestured towards the table. With his big smile, he made the gesture seem extra special. Willis proceeded to pull out a chair for Laura, then took the opposite chair for himself.

As luck would have it, their table was located in a very quiet corner of the restaurant. It was almost like they had their own private dining room. As they perused the menu, which was heavy on the Italian side, the waiter came over and asked if they would like a drink. Willis looked at Laura and asked, "What are you in the mood for? Do you want a drink, or shall we just have some wine?"

"Oh, I don't know. I'm not great at making up my mind these days." There was a pause and then she finally said, "How about having a cocktail and then follow it with a nice bottle of Pinot... Would that work for you?"

"Sure, Laura, This night's for you. What would you like?"

"Make mine a Lemon Drop Martini with a sugar rim, please."

The waiter nodded and looked at Willis with an inquisitive look to which Willis responded, "I'll have a Johnnie Walker Black Label on the rocks, please."

The waiter nodded, handed them each a menu, and

said, "I'll be right back with your drinks, folks."

And so they settled in, and with a sigh, Laura said, "Ah, this is so nice. It's so calm and peaceful here. I could use an emotional vacation if there is such a thing. It's been so hard to relax and be able to focus these days. I don't understand but I seem to be of two minds these days... That is, I'm so worried that people are getting killed here but on the other hand I can't believe it's really happening. It's all so distressing and confusing."

Willis looked at her with affection and concern. She had always been such a special friend of his mother's, so caring and loving towards others, but Willis was now feeling a new warmth and concern for her, a warmth which was—to his surprise—also physical. He was more and more attracted to her. *Hmmm*, he thought, *this is something I didn't expect!*

Laura looked at him with affection and said, "I heard you on the phone yesterday talking to either Ross or Monty, I'm not sure which, but anyway it sounded like you were discussing the purchasing of a piece of property. Is this something you've done before?"

"Well, yes, I thought I had mentioned it to you earlier... it was something Ross came up with. The boys and I seem to have a knack for finding properties that are inexpensive... like a foreclosure or a property that a bank has ended up with for a variety of reasons and they want to unload it. If one has a good eye, and we seem to, one can get a real bargain, buy it, fix it up by giving it a fresh paint job, some new carpeting, and possibly new appliances, and then sell it. To date, the few houses we've bought and fixed up have all sold at a sizable profit."

Laura looked at Willis and smiled. *Who would have thought this man and his "sons" would be so clever? Hmmm, another side to him*, she mused.

Soon the waiter brought them their drinks, and they sat quietly perusing the menu as they were in no rush. Eventually, they settled on the Chicken Marsala for Laura and the Veal Parmesan for Willis. When prompted by the waiter, they ordered another round of drinks even though they had a bottle of wine on order. Laura soon mellowed out and Willis took the opportunity to ask some questions.

"I'm curious about all the interesting folks I've met since I arrived. I found Else to be fascinating, as she has obviously a self-made woman and very successful. "What's your take on her Laura?"

"I'm not sure. She seems to be such a combination of traits... Mostly aimed at being successful. She must have been a terror when she was younger and out in the work force. Even with her being retired, I doubt that she is capable of just relaxing. With her, everything is a competition. She's even in competition with herself. I've known her, say—what, maybe three or so years now and as far as I can see, she's never worn the same outfit. It's like she has to prove that she is the best, has the best and has to best everyone. Odd, isn't it?"

"There have been a few times when someone upset her or disagreed with her and I have to tell you, her reaction wasn't pretty. She can be terrifying. If one has a disagreement with her, she doesn't listen to your point of view, she just overrides you with that strong assertive manner of hers, you know with that Danish accent of hers. Once Claudine crossed her over something dumb, I can't even remember what it was about, but Else was ready to kill her! Not a pleasant moment, I can tell you. Not the usual behavior for us here at Sunningdale."

"What about Bruton?" Willis asked.

"Some say he has a drinking problem... Sad about his wife. It's kind of sweet how he dotes on those ducks... a strange substitution for her but, hey, to each his own."

Willis took a sip of his wine and said, "Now I really enjoyed meeting the two ladies Felicia and Matty. I found Felicia to be very nice, very agreeable, and amazingly attractive."

Laura gave Willis a knowing look and said, "I think every man around here thinks that, even the gay ones... Maybe especially the gay ones."

"Why is that?" Willis asked.

"Oh, I don't know… I think there might be a special appreciation on their part for a woman such as Felicia, as they often respect style, class, and taste."

"Well, that means you'd definitely be on their 'appreciation list'," said Willis with a smile.

"But what was your take on Matty?" she asked. "I think she's exceptionally smart, very astute. Did you get that impression?"

"Well, it's clear that she's certainly smart. The question is how smart? If I'm to find out what's going on here in Sunningdale maybe I'd best talk Matty up a bit." Why he avoided telling her that he had already met with her was a mystery to Willis. Why was he hiding facts from Laura from time to time?

Laura nodded her head in agreement and then went on to say, "Now Hal… I have such a feeling of concern for him. I can't begin to fathom what needing a heart transplant would be like. I saw him earlier today and he's now using a cane to get around… Something about a shoulder problem. Awful! And to think, he was once a highly sought after basketball player. What a terrible thing to happen to such a nice, fine man. From what I've heard, he plans to live life to its fullest as best he can. What would you do, Willis, if you felt there was a good chance that you might not survive for long?"

Willis wondered if Laura wasn't really asking the question about herself. "Hard to imagine. My guess is I'd…You know, I'm not sure." was his only response to her question. He then went on to say, "When I was with Bruton earlier, he mentioned the terrible accident that Roz O' Connor had when she fell while carrying a knife and somehow managed to cut herself so severely that she bled to death. He's not convinced it was just a mishap. Do you think it was an accident or could she have been murdered?"

Laura played with the stem of her martini glass, looked shocked, and finally said, "God, I… I just don't know. We all supposed that it was one of those terrible, freak accidents. I never thought of it any other way. The police of course were summoned, and they all thought that it was, as I said, just a terrible accident... you know, just an awful situation. Can we get on a more pleasant subject please?"

'Oh, I'm sorry. Initially you were the one who urged me to come to Sunningdale because you said, and I quote you, 'Strange things have been happening around here.' You had mentioned that there were other mysterious deaths such as Herb Talmon and two others. So, what's it to be, Laura? Search out the truth or bury it?"

"Oh, Willis, I just don't know. I'm so confused and conflicted. Part of me thinks it's all a series of crazy accidents and part of me strangely feels that there's a murderer here in Sunningdale and he or she must be stopped. Please… Please help me! I don't like what's happening here and what it's doing to me. I don't know what to do. I'm frightened, puzzled, and alarmed… I just want to shut down."

Willis took her hand and tried to comfort her. As they had now started to drink the wine, he wondered if maybe their drinking had loosened her tongue or had just plain confused her.

He decided to change the subject to comfort her but, at the same time, it worried him. Something was going on here and it just didn't seem to make sense. *Damned if I can totally figure it out!* he thought, *but I have an inkling and it bothers and scares the hell out of me. That research I did earlier is giving me an important clue and I don't like it… I'm getting really worried!*

After a short quiet spell, the waiter came by and poured each another glass of wine and brought them their dinners. Willis proceeded to ask her again, "What was your childhood like?" thinking a change in subject might be welcomed.

There was a long pause, and Willis wondered if he had inadvertently touched on a nerve, but Laura sat there quietly and finally said, "You know, your mother and I used to share our most intimate thoughts. I certainly miss that. Her death left me sort of adrift with no one to confide in."

Willis paused and sort of held his breath. Maybe Laura might confide in him as a sort of surrogate version of his mother. Also, he thought the drinks might have loosened her tongue a bit. He certainly hoped so.

After a remarkably long pause, where Willis thought Laura had bailed out of the conversation, she suddenly looked him in the eye and said, "I've never told a soul about the shock I experienced when I was five years old. Not even your mother. It was buried deep within me for years but lately, and I mean VERY recently, it's starting to come to the surface. I'm starting to recall details that I've always hid… remembrances that have always been so embarrassing. Things that deeply traumatized me."

There was a long pause when Willis thought, *I wonder if she'll be able to continue...* To his relief she did. Letting out a huge sigh, Laura proceeded to say: "When I was five, as I've told you, I was a striking beautiful child. I know because there were all those photos of me during that period. Hmmm, yeah, I know… how things change!"

Willis started to interrupt her to say that she was still beautiful, but Laura waved him off indicating don't bother… don't interrupt me. She went on to say, "The interesting thing was the transition I went through during that time."

There was a long pause, as it was apparent that Laura was trying to clear her mind and decide if she should go ahead with her story and, if so, how much to tell and how to tell it.

Some time passed and she finally said, "I had an uncle, Uncle Conrad… you know, the man I've mentioned to you… my mother's brother. He was a very close to the family…. Very close to us. He spent a lot of time at our home…. He used to fuss over me. You know, saying how beautiful I was, how charming and so forth. Well, one night…"

She paused as though it was too difficult to go further. Willis sat there very still and waited to see where this would go. Finally, after a long delay, Laura said, in almost a little child's voice, "He was babysitting me and….and he… he hurt me."

Willis sat there frozen, unable to move.

"I felt so ashamed. What he was doing to me I knew was wrong but I didn't know how to stop him. I know it sounds stupid, but I felt culpable… Guilty. That I was somehow responsible… That… that I had caused this to happen. Of course, I now know I was in no way at fault, but to this day I just can't stop feeling guilty,"

After a long pause, Willis ventured to ask, "What did you do? How on earth did you cope?"

"I pulled myself into a safety cocoon. I hid my shame and fear. Strangely in the process, I lost my ability to speak for a long, long time. I used to pretend that I was someone else. Maybe I still do to this day, I'm not sure." After a long pause, Laura went on to say, "I eventually slowly started to speak again...I kind of rejoined the human race."

After a long pause, she continued, "You know, I never had children. It was a clear decision on my part as I never wanted a child of mine to go through what I had gone through. No, I was determined that no child of mine would EVER be abused. It's been a long and painful journey, this life, but I'm kind of proud that I've survived it. Shortly after this terrible time and when I became mute, my father somehow figured out what had happened. He never said a word to either me or to my mother but from what I can gather it was then that he and Uncle Conrad went out in that canoe, and it tipped over and Uncle Conrad drowned. I'm sure Dad arranged that. Scary, eh? Hard to imagine someone killing another person..."

They sat in silence, each in his own thoughts. Willis was at a loss as to what to say. This went on for a while until the waiter came by and, in his bubbly voice, asked if there was anything else they might like. Willis wondered what Laura would have asked for if she could have anything she wanted, but she seemingly had closed the subject, and apparently that was it for the evening. Without finishing the meal, she asked for the check. Willis grabbed it and paid it and they soon were walking home arm in arm, both deep in their own thoughts.

As they reached home, Laura was once again her old self, laughing, saying how silly she had been. "Forget what I said earlier." She had clearly shut down, probably never to broach that subject again. However, It was clear that the drinks had not only loosened her tongue, but they had also strangely awakened a physical need in her. Maybe the revelation on Laura's part had released a physical hunger in her and that, in turn, had instilled an awareness in Willis.

Suddenly on impulse Laura kissed him, first gently, but then with a ferocious appetite which Willis—to his surprise—willingly returned.

It was as if the drinking had unlocked a door within each of them with similar results. Soon they were in her bedroom. She turned the lights down low and they started to slowly remove each other's clothing. It was hot and very sensual as they lowered themselves onto her bed. *This woman is amazing, so sensual, so exciting I never knew... so changeable,* he thought. She in turn felt suddenly safe, cared for, and it was thrilling. And a new chapter for both of them began...

Sunday—Day Five
A disturbing thought begins to grow

Eight o'clock that next morning, Willis's head was spinning with thoughts as he slipped out of Laura's bed and returned to his room. While the evening had been extremely exciting, Willis was beginning to get an idea of what might actually be happening in the full picture of things, and it greatly disturbed him. The more he thought about it, the more convinced he was that he might be on the right track, and that he should be careful not to allow himself to be sidetracked or emotionally compromised.

He checked his cell phone, then hooked it up to charge, as he had not gotten around to charging it the night before. He next laid out some clothes for the day, went to get a cup of coffee and saw Laura already in the backyard, once again in her white terrycloth robe with its white belt that accentuated her tiny waist, sitting in a recliner, drinking coffee, and reading the newspaper. The watering can for her beloved bonsai plant was on the table nearby.

She seemed occupied, so he decided to play it safe and just wave a "good morning" and go back to his room where he showered, shaved, and dressed. When he walked into the kitchen, he found his breakfast laid out for him. There was a box of cereal, some English muffins, a selection of three different types of jam, a frying pan, and a note saying:

Dear Willis,

I had to go out… so sorry. There's milk in the refrigerator, also eggs if you feel up to cooking them.

I've gone over to Hal Snyder's place, you know the guy who needs a heart transplant. He's having trouble getting around so I'm dropping off some food for him.

Also, I'm going over to Rebecca's to check in on her. She might want to go to church and if so I'll take her there but I'll be back ASAP!

Enjoy the morning. Needless to say, I enjoyed last night!
Love, Laura

Willis stared at the note for a while. He found her consideration charming. It had been a very long time since someone of the opposite sex had intrigued him. That, and the signature "Love, Laura" made him remarkably happy. Happier than he had been in quite some time. He stood there barely moving, as a sudden realization swept through his whole being. Was this the beginning of love? He truly didn't know, as it had been ages since he had felt for a woman as he now did for Laura.

After a while, he filled his mug, popped an English muffin in the toaster, and proceeded to pick up his cell phone to check in with his assistants Ross and Monty to see how their latest case was shaping up, and just to say, "Hi". Was he avoiding this new thought or was he in need of a break from the thoughts he was having? Ross and Monty were like the sons he never had. He missed the two of them and they might be an excellent diversion, as he wanted a distraction from the amazing thoughts he was having!

When Ross answered the phone, he said, "What's up, Dad?", having seen the caller ID on his phone screen. While Ross was, in reality, not his son, they had bonded and because Ross had no father, he had taken to fondly referring to

Willis as "Dad." When Willis started to talk, Ross said, "Hold on for a second, Dad my super smart brother Monty is coming into the room here and I want to put you on the speaker."

Willis loved the "smart" joke, as they were twins and identical in so many ways, including being "super smart".

Monty promptly chimed in with, "Hi there, how's it going, Willis?" Monty had a dad, so he treated Willis like a favorite uncle of sorts. "How's Laura?" Both men were very interested in Willis finding a companion. Someone to share his life with.

Willis smiled and quicky changed the subject by saying, "Knowing your attraction to mysteries, you'd love it here. There are so many interesting folks who live here and, sad to say, it looks like there's a big-time murderer on the loose and I've got to deal with the problem before more people get hurt."

"Do you know who the killer is, Dad?" asked Ross.

"Not sure, but I have a really strong hunch and it's not pleasant, not pleasant at all. I just hope I'm wrong and if I'm not, I hope I can stop the killer before anyone else gets hurt."

"How are you going to stop him, Dad?"

"Ah, as they used to say, 'That's the sixty-four thousand dollar question,' a phrase that's waaaay before your time!"

Willis heard the twins chuckle, which made him smile, but also feel a bit old as it involved a scandal in the 1950s and, yeah, even before his time… something his father had once told him about.

He had planned to talk through what was going on here at Sunningdale, but he wanted to do some more research to confirm his theory before laying it out for them. And so, after discussing the boys' latest case, Willis resisted giving the boys his fatherly advice and, instead, signed off, had a bite of breakfast, got into his exercise outfit, ran a couple of miles—which was his normal practice as he wanted to keep in shape—then showered, made a few calls, and worked on some notes. In a way he was avoiding going on the internet to research his theory, as he was deeply concerned about what he might find.

A little after noon Laura showed up. She was all smiles, smartly dressed in a very "up" pink and green patterned dress with shoes and purse that matched the green. She gave him a kiss before proceeding to say that she saw Hal and he seemed to be doing a bit better, but was depressed by the complexity of getting a heart transplant and now his shoulder problem. "That poor man!"

She went on to say that she had then driven Rebecca to church, and that after church she had dropped her off, parked the car, and while walking back after having parked the car, she ran into Tony and he was kind of all riled up. "I prodded him to tell me what was disturbing him, but he ducked the question which, needless to say, bothered me. When pressed, Tony told me in a very strained voice that he was going to see Carl Stone, the head of Plymouth Harbor." He then said, and I quote him, 'Believe me I have some really interesting information to give him.' With that he stormed off as best as a 96-year-old man could, as Tony is quite fragile. I wonder if he realizes that it's Sunday and Carl won't be in his office?"

This turn of events clearly had bothered Laura, and also Willis. Willis tactfully decided to change the subject and said, "What was that business about a Valentine's Day party that the ladies were discussing the other night?

"Oh that, they were talking about Crayton. You haven't met him yet, but you will. He's putting together another Valentine's Day party. He did one four years ago and it was such a big hit, that he's been doing it every year since."

Gesturing for her to sit, Willis said, "Tell me about the party and what Crayton is like."

Laura quickly sat down and appeared to grab onto the subject like it was a life preserver of sorts and said, "Well, the party is really fabulous. It originally started off as just a cocktail party on Valentine's Day, but each year Crayton tries to outdo the previous year to the point that last year, he had giant heart-shaped red balloons all around Holmby Hall where the party is held. He also requested that everyone wear either red, white or black outfits or a combination of the three colors and it turned out to be a sensational idea… very festive. Everyone loved it and got into the fun of it."

"Crayton had red invitations made in the shape of hearts that stated the place, time and the wardrobe requirement with the stipulation that anyone who didn't adhere to the wardrobe requirement would not be admitted. Wouldn't you know, but then maybe not, as you don't know Hal, but Hal showed up in jeans and a tan shirt with an 'I don't give a fig what Crayton wants' attitude and there was quite the scene when Hal was asked to leave. Actually, it was more Crayton ordering Hal to leave. It got quite ugly and Hal swore that he'd get even. To tell you the truth, I thought Hal was way out of line and I hated that Hal threatened Crayton."

"What's Crayton like?" asked Willis.

There was a long pause and finally Laura said, "Well, he's fun, smart, a bit over the top and he's gay."

"How do people here feel about his being gay? Does everyone know it?"

"Well, let's put it this way, even Helen Keller would know he's gay. He's just kinda a bit outrageous. But I should add, he's fun, smart, really rich, and generous to a fault. He's usually very kind too, although not to Hal after last year's party."

"Does everyone generally like Crayton?"

"Generally, I would say yes, and those who are less enthusiastic about him or down and out anti-gay can just keep their mouths shut. Believe me, parties like the ones Crayton throws are few and far between around here, and folks here generally appreciate his creative and generous nature and want to be a part of it. That is, everyone except Hal… and knowing Hal, one worries a bit that he might try to harm Crayton."

"You say Crayton is rich... How rich?"

"Well, let's just say, as an only child, he came from a wealthy family and then he had a distant cousin with whom he reportedly had a 'special' relationship, and the guy left him an enormous amount of money, much to the consternation of some of the guy's relatives. I'm not sure it's true, but I heard that the cousin had been the initial beneficiary of the man who invented the zipper, and the saying from the disgruntled relatives is that Crayton has been opening them ever since!" Laura said this with a wink of her eye.

Willis loved the humor of that, and wished Laura could consistently find humor in her life. It was strange how she seemed to enjoy life one moment and then not be up next. *Very changeable, that woman, especially when one thought of what had transpired last night. All very strange and odd...*

Later that afternoon, Willis decided to take yet another walk, as they were proving to be extraordinarily productive in the strangest ways. He decided on a whim, to head around the pond. On one of the paths, he found Tony sitting on a bench looking strangely distracted and dejected. Not knowing Tony very well, Willis ventured "Mind if I join you? It's such a nice day, I decided to take a walk."

When there was no reply from Tony, Willis tried another tack. He sat down next to Tony and asked, "Are you all right? You seem distracted or maybe even a bit dejected." It was a wild guess on Willis's part but, apparently, he hit the nail on the head as Tony let out a huge sigh but said, "I really don't want to talk about it."

Willis let a little time go by and then finally said, "Want to try telling me what's going on? I'm a good listener."

Tony looked at him with a mixture of surprise and distrust, but said nothing.

Willis waited a minute and then said, "I'm no psychologist but I can tell that you're disturbed. If I can be of some help..." And he left it at that.

Tony sighed and finally said, "I just came from Carl Stone's office; you know the guy who runs Sunningdale. We have a real problem here and I wanted to alert him to it, but I forgot that it's Sunday and there was no one there except the receptionist at the front desk. I asked her to get Carl on the phone, but she said to her knowledge he was out of town today and that whatever my problem was it could wait until tomorrow. In truth, I'd bet he's more involved in expanding this place to the point that he's pushed the deaths around here off to the side. What a mess." He said, "Believe me, they'll regret it... Everyone will."

"Want to tell me about it?"

"I really don't want to discuss it." There was a long pause and then with a deep sigh Tony said, "I guess it can't hurt. If you're really involved in trying to solve what's going on here in Sunningdale, then I suggest you go on the Internet and check out DID—dissociative identity disorder. Cleveland Clinic has done some interesting work on this subject." With that, Tony got up, sighed, and slowly walked away.

Willis sat there, trying to figure out what Tony had just said... *Maybe I was just handed another piece of the puzzle, an important one I should think, but how does it fit in?*

Later, Willis came back to the house to find Laura in the study, composing a letter and deep in thought. Willis waited for her to look up, but she was so deeply concentrated on composing the letter that she seemed unaware of his presence. Finally, Willis said, "I don't want to disturb you, but would you like a cup of tea?"

When Laura looked up she seemed distant… removed. She finally said, "Okay, that would be really nice." It was like she was returning from some place far away in her head. Willis went into the kitchen, made a pot of tea, and while the water was boiling, he found some biscuits in the pantry and set them out on a plate. He also managed to find a tray and arranged everything on it. When the tea was ready, he brought it into the study and set it on the coffee table.

"Your tea awaits you Madame," he announced, trying to add a little humor to lighten what seemed like a somewhat heavy atmosphere. Laura, with a tentative smile, joined him on the sofa as he quietly poured some tea for both of them. Luckily, no one wanted lemon, as he hadn't been able to find any in the fridge and he wasn't about to go over to Claudine's yard to pick one from her tree of many fruits. Besides, he had already removed the fruit from the trees as a precaution. And so, they quietly had their tea.

At one point Willis said, "I ran into Tony on the way here. He mentioned something about DID. I plan to look it up on the Internet. It's short for dissociative identity disorder. Do you know anything about that? Tony seemed to think it's related to the deaths around here. Any thoughts on this?"

Laura looked up from the book she was reading and shrugged, "No, I'm afraid not," and she returned to her book.

Willis sensed that Laura was being evasive about the subject.

After a while, Willis excused himself and went to his room, fired up his computer, and typed in "DID—dissociative identity disorder" and spent a fascinating time exploring a possible new piece to the puzzle. He discovered that DID was a very rare mental condition where a person has two or more separate identities. These personalities control a person's behavior at different times. Each identity has its own personal history, traits, likes, and dislikes. DID can lead to gaps in memory and hallucinations (believing something is real when it isn't). DID is usually the result of sexual or physical abuse during childhood. It's a way for the person to distance or detach himself from the trauma.

This gave him a great deal to think about, and since he was accustomed to doing his best thinking while on a walk, he left and was gone for close to an hour. Later when he returned, Laura asked, "I know we recently had tea, but it was really a light fare. Any thoughts about dinner tonight? I'm not terribly hungry but we ought to eat something. How about you?"

"Oh, I'm fine...Not very hungry myself either. What do you have in mind?"

"I thought maybe we could just have some soup, fruit, and I have quite a nice selection of cheese in the refrigerator if that would suit you."

"That'd be fine with me."

"Good, I'll take the cheese out now so it can get to room temperature and we can eat in, say, an hour or so. I know it's probably early for you, especially since we just had tea, but I'm suddenly very tired and thought I'd like to have an early dinner and then go to bed at a decent hour for a change."

"Actually, that would be perfect. I failed to mention that I had bought a few bottles of wine while I was out the other day, so if you're okay with a bottle of *Amarone della Valpolicella* we'd be all set."

Laura replied, "Lovely." She got up, grabbed a pair of clippers and went out into the yard and Willis followed her. She quickly and efficiently cut a selection of flowers "for the dining room table." As she did this, she mentioned that she had just seen Bruton walking Rebecca's dog for her. "Isn't that thoughtful of him to help her? He certainly gets around. He seems to be everywhere."

"Yeah, but if pressed, I'd prefer to say he's a beehive of inactivity!"

As she walked past Willis, he detected an amazingly charming and delicate perfume which she had on and said, "That perfume you're wearing is amazing… so special!"

Laura broke into a smile and said, "I'm so glad you

noticed It. It's one of my few indulgences." With that, she said, "I'll be right back" and quickly went to her room and brought back an attractive but small, simple squarish bottle with a gold cap. She held up the bottle and proceeded to say, "I had to get the bottle because of its long, complicated name." She turned the bottle towards the light and read the name on it and said, "It's called Maison Francis Kurkdjian—I'm not sure if that's the correct pronunciation… The rest of the name is: 'Baccarat Rouge 540 Extrait de Parfum.' I told you it was long!" she said with a smile and went on to say, "It's alarmingly expensive but I love it. I feel the need to indulge myself a little bit these days. There's only one place that carries it and that's Herbarium here in Sarasota. Lucky for me they know it as just 'Maison Francis.'"

Willis smiled, as it was wonderful to see her a bit pleased, even if it was just for the moment.

Then, as they were going into the house, they saw Bruton walk by, saying, "Come on Charma, let's not take forever, we need to get you home to Rebecca." Willis wondered if Bruton had been eavesdropping on their conversation. It certainly looked that way.

Willis and Laura went into the house, and Laura proceeded to fill a crystal vase with water, arrange the flowers in it, and place it on the dining room table. She then proceeded to show Willis a plastic container of split pea soup. As she started to open it, she mentioned, "I bought it at Morton's. It's a high-end gourmet grocery store here in town. It's not quite on the same level as the perfume bottle I just showed you but it's usually very good. Well... perhaps not quite up to the standards of your mother's cooking, but it'll do."

She soon started heating it up while Willis helped by unwrapping the selection of cheeses and then setting out two placemats, some wine glasses, as well as water glasses which he filled from a special tap by the sink. He also went to his room and brought back the bottle of wine he had mentioned earlier. He asked where she kept the opener, and she directed him to the top drawer of one of the kitchen cabinets with a nod of her head saying, top drawer. Soon he had the wine opened so it could breathe.

Willis looked at the bottle and said, "I know it's old fashioned, but I really dislike these new twist top bottles. There's something… I don't know, charming about the ritual of uncorking a bottle of wine, especially if the wine is special like I hope this one will be.

Laura smiled in agreement. As it was getting to be dusk, she set out several candles which were in candle sticks. "Do you like these candlesticks Willis? I bought them on a trip I made to Capri with you mother a number of years ago.

"Ah, I have the identical pair at home. Mom must have bought them on the same trip with you." Willis proceeded to think, *It's almost like having the old Laura back. I wonder where she's been.* He proceeded to say, "Being here with you, Laura, has been in a way a gift."

Laura looked up and smiled in surprise. It was probably the first real smile he had seen from her since his arrival other than the night before.

"I'm really enjoying this moment. Thank you Laura."

"I'm enjoying it too Willis. More than you probably realize." She thought for a moment and then asked, "What's your life like these days?"

"Well, as you know from Mom, I'm divorced. Not sure I fully understand why but it is what it is.... My wife and I just stopped communicating and sort of drifted apart, first mentally and then finally physically, compliments of a divorce she instigated. So now it's no wife, no attachments. Maybe it was just meant to be, and possibly it's a good thing too, I don't know. I'm getting on and I can honestly say after the divorce, I was pretty soured on the idea of any sort of relationship." With this he grinned uncomfortably.

"I was really okay with the idea of no kids… no involvements. However, through some rather extraordinary events I met Monty and Ross, the twin gentlemen you've heard me talk about. They've in a way become my surrogate family… my kids. They're smart, interesting and wonderfully supportive." He looked out the window and said, "I love 'em. I consider myself to be very lucky, very lucky indeed.“

"Hmm, I wish I could say the same," Laura replied. "I don't know... After my husband died, life changed for me, which is to be expected, I suppose, but it's been strange. There's just no other word for it.“

There was a long pause. Finally, Willis said, "I ran into Tony earlier today and he appeared to be greatly disturbed."

"What on earth about?" Laura asked curiously.

"I'm not sure, but he said he had gone to see Carl Stone about something… something VERY important."

"And?" asked Laura anxiously

"Damned if I know. Tony apparently wasn't successful about seeing Carl as it's Sunday and Carl's office was closed. He was told by the receptionist at the front desk to come back tomorrow. Tony wouldn't or couldn't tell me what it was all about. He was very vague. For some reason I don't think he fully trusted me. All very strange. In any case, Carl is supposedly going to see him tomorrow."

"Hmmm," said Laura and appeared to kind of mull over the thought.

They finished their soup and cheese and, after a dessert of vanilla ice cream with some hot fudge over it, which Laura had quickly and efficiently heated up, Laura announced, "I hope you don't mind but I set up a small group to come here tomorrow for a game of dominoes. Would you like to join us?"

"Sure, I haven't played that game since I can't remember when, but it sounds like fun."

"Good." After a pause, she said, "I think I'll go to bed early. I'm not sure why I'm so tired these days. I hope I'm not coming down with a cold."

And so, Willis got up, gave her a light kiss and said, "Don't mind about the dishes. I'll take care of them."

"Oh, that's so caring. Your mother did a good job of bringing you up, Willis." She smiled affectionately at him and started for her room but suddenly turned back and impulsively gave him a tender hug before going to her room.

Later, as Willis was getting ready for bed, he thought that he might have heard the back door open and close, but he wasn't sure and kind of dismissed it, as he was listening to the news and thought it probably was just his imagination.

Monday—Day Six
A disturbing aftermath

Once again Willis, being an early riser, was up and in the kitchen, but to his surprise there was no coffee set up. In the past, Laura had always put out a coffee mug plus set the coffee machine to "start". So, Willis went to the fridge as he had seen Laura do, got out the coffee and tried to make a pot. It proved to be difficult as Laura's coffee machine was totally different from the one he had at home.

He shrugged, took some jam and butter plus an English muffin out of the fridge, cut one of them open and popped the two halves in the toaster while he turned the TV on low as not to disturb Laura, as it looked like she was sleeping in. *I hope she was wrong about coming down with a cold,* he thought, but then she came out of her room fully dressed and not in her usual robe.

Without saying a word, she went over to the cabinet that housed the mugs, grabbed one and, when she saw that she had not prepared coffee in advance, she proceeded to make a pot. There was no talk, she just picked up the newspaper from the front door stoop, and when the coffee was ready, she proceeded to pour a cup of coffee for herself. Strangely she did not pour one for Willis. Very odd.

Hmmm, thought Willis, *That's different. She always shows up in the morning in her bathrobe, is pleasant right off the bat, has coffee and then goes and gets dressed.*

Laura seemed to finally connect with the day and with Willis. She took down a coffee cup, poured him a cup, left it in front of him and proceeded to take the watering can and went out to water her beloved bonsai tree. Upon returning she finally said, "Good morning. I hope you slept well, Willis."

Willis took a sip of his coffee and said, "Yes, just fine. How about you?"

"Oh, okay, I guess. Just too much on my mind."

"If I'm not being too nosey... like what? Is there anything I can do help you?"

Laura seemed to think about his offer and replied, "Don't I wish, but no, I don't think you can help me with what's bothering me. But thanks." And with that she put the watering can away and headed towards her part of the villa. He assumed she was getting ready to leave for the day. He pondered, *I wonder what's in store for us today?*

He was soon to find out.

When Laura finally emerged, Willis had the odd feeling that she had been waiting for him to leave. *Maybe I'm getting in the way, overstaying my welcome. Not sure why, as we certainly had a pleasant dinner last night. I don't know...* and he left it at that.

Suddenly the phone rang, and Laura picked it up. She listened for a while and then said, "Oh no! It can't be. Are you absolutely a hundred percent sure? Oh God! What's happening here?"

After a long pause, he heard her say, "I'm so sorry. This is devastating news. I have to hang up. I'm so upset."

She sat down on the sofa and held her head as she bent over, apparently trying to catch her breath.

Willis gently asked, "What's the matter Laura? What's happening?

She looked up at Willis and said, "He's dead… Tony's dead!" And she bent over and quietly wept.

"What happened? Did he have a heart attack?"

There was a long pause and then she said quietly, "No, he was... He was murdered!"

"How?" Willis finally asked. "Are you sure?"

"That was Matty who called. She told me that she had gone over to give him some fudge she had made for him. When Tony didn't answer his door, she asked one of the caretakers to check in on him, as she had arranged yesterday to drop off the fudge this morning. She waited for the caretaker to drive by in one of the golf carts they use to take people around here. When he finally arrived, he took out a pass key and they went in and found him. Tony had apparently been strangled with a white cord of some sort, which was still tightly tied around his throat when they found him. That poor man!"

Later, Laura said to Willis, "Earlier I said we'd play Mexican Train, you know, dominoes this afternoon. I thought it might be a bit of a distraction from what is going on here, but somehow it seems disrespectful towards Tony to play a game after what just happened."

"I don't know" said Willis, "Maybe it would help everyone deal with it if they could take their minds off of this for a while. Kind of give folks a breather."

There was a pause, and finally Laura said, "Maybe you're right. Let me call the others and see how they feel."

"Oh, who all might be coming?" asked Willis.

"A few folks you haven't met yet and might find interesting. Let's see, there's Les, Kathy, and Philip," she said with sort of a frown "Plus Karl and Rebecca. You'll like those last two." I'll give 'em all a call and see if they're up for it." And with that Laura left the room and Willis could hear her making the phone calls.

Apparently, everyone liked the idea of getting the tragedy off their minds, at least for a few hours, and it was agreed that they would all meet at Laura's at 2:00 just after lunch. That way Laura wouldn't have to prepare a lunch for everyone.

Laura made a quick run to the store, as she felt that even though everyone would have eaten, maybe she should have a decent selection of nibbles other than just pretzels and nuts. Willis took the time to review some notes and, more importantly, do some research on a theory he had.

An hour before the guests were to arrive, Laura started to take out the peanut butter-covered pretzels and an assortment of nuts. She then put Willis to work making up some nibbles with what Willis called "a mystery spread" that both Laura and his mother used to make for occasions like this. The only difference was Laura used the spread it on Ritz crackers and Willis's mother had used a rectangular cracker of sorts. At the last minute, Laura grabbed a large plastic container of M&Ms, which she had Willis put some in a crystal serving dish.

Since everyone wasn't due for twenty or so minutes, Laura took the time to tell Willis something about the guests. She smiled as she thought of Karl and Rebecca. "Karl and Rebecca are two of my favorite people here at Sunningdale. Their background is both wonderful and, sorry to say, not so wonderful. They've been married for, hmm probably about 20 years now. Karl was a famous impresario in the opera world and Rebecca was on her way to being a really fabulous and famous opera singer. Apparently, she had a remarkable voice. Their life was golden until one day Karl had one of those days where there was too much to do and not enough time."

"He needed to get a musical score delivered to someone very important and he was unable to get a service that was available to make the delivery on time. Consequently, Rebecca offered to run the score over. She drove over to the address that Karl had given her and when she went to park the car in an underground garage, two thugs attacked her, thinking there was something valuable in the briefcase she was carrying. One grabbed her from behind with his arm tightly wrapped around her throat while his buddy grabbed the briefcase. In the struggle, the stranglehold the one had on her was so tight that her vocal cords were severely hurt."

"The thugs were never caught, but the really sad thing is Rebecca's voice was damaged beyond repair. While she can talk and, in general, has nearly the full use of her vocal cords, she totally lost her ability to sing beautifully. However, Rebecca is a remarkable woman... Very resourceful and positive in her thinking. What she did was become a superb vocal coach who was and still is to this day in great demand."

"For a long time, Karl was greatly disturbed and felt he was responsible for Rebecca's great loss. Since Karl is considerably older than Rebecca, he has retired and devotes himself to keeping her happy. Rebecca, on the other hand, continues to work but is very selective with who she takes on, and that way she keeps her workload down. I think you'll find that they are delightful people, as they exude warmth and love towards each other and the people who come into their lives."

The other three people who are coming are, how shall I put it? Well, they're another story... There's Kathy. Nothing seems to really bother or at least penetrate her general sense of serenity. She's just sweet and I'm kind of protective of her. Now the two men in her life... well, you'll see. I guess in retrospect maybe I shouldn't have invited them, but I feel sorry for Kathy. I think you'll find her to be quite attractive and really sweet. Of the three, she's the one who is the happiest, the most agreeable. I like her or maybe I just feel sorry for her."

"Coming with her is her son Philip, who is a piece of work. Then there's Leo, her so-called husband. Now Leo's an interesting story. I'll be very interested in your take on him. He was married to Sonny who lived in the tower. She was a wealthy widow. They met on a cruise, and he swept her off her feet. She was crazy in love with him, and he moved in with her. I'm not sure what his background is but I suspect he didn't have much money."

"Well, they got married, had a big wedding here in Sunningdale's chapel, and went on to live the high life… trips, cruises, totally redecorated their apartment. Even bought a yacht and housed it at the Yacht Club. Unfortunately, about a year and a half into the marriage, they went on yet another cruise. This time to the Orient. While there, she suffered a condition that was never fully explained, and she died. Leo opted to have her body cremated there. and he returned to Sunningdale sadder but richer, as one might say."

"Leo continued to live here and is very social, as has been his custom. He soon met Kathy, who is very rich, beautiful, a southern belle with an accent you could cut with a knife. She's very sweet but, as the saying goes, she's not the brightest bulb around. She lives in one of the six penthouses, is very rich, and tends to travel around the country by hiring private jets at about $80,000 a shot…

and is conveniently a widow. It hasn't been that long since they met but Leo and Kathy appear to be quite inseparable, much to her son's, Philip's dismay."

"The general gossip is that Philip, who is quite the operator himself, had been counting on living on Kathy's money both now and after she passes away. He's determined that Leo won't get the chance to get her to change her estate to totally benefit Leo and totally cut out Philip. Philip's work on sabotaging their relationship to date has been quite unsuccessful, as Kathy is wildly in love with Leo and relishes all the attention he's showering on her."

"Just last month, Leo and Kathy took a short cruise in the Bahamas and announced that they had been married by the captain of the ship during the cruise. Philip didn't waste any time and was able to ascertain that the marriage was a sham, that the idea of a captain conducting a marriage on a ship, while romantic, is not legit unless the captain is legally authorized to conduct such a marriage."

"Philip quickly proved that the captain, while well-meaning, had misrepresented his right to perform such a ceremony. This did not go over well with Leo, and it left Kathy totally confused. To say there is bad blood between the two men would be a huge understatement. Meanwhile, Philip is keeping close tabs on his mother, much to the considerable annoyance of Leo and to Kathy's uncertainty."

"Hmmm," said Willis. "It'll be interesting to see who wins that battle."

Within moments, the doorbell rang, and Laura let Leo, Kathy, and Philip in. Clearly Leo and Philip must have just had words, as Kathy was saying with her southern drawl, "I just don't understand why y'all can't get along"... Followed by dead silence accented with glaring between the two men!

Kathy was petite and was wearing an outfit that was much too young for her… tight fitting and appropriate for a woman half her age. Leo was tall, dark, and sported a closely trimmed beard and a smile that came too frequently and often at inappropriate moments. It often looked like it was the result of unseen nervousness and it gave him an almost sinister, oily quality like that of a handsome villain in an old movie. His black pants and shirt didn't help matters.

Philip, in contrast was blonde, had very pale skin and colorless clothes to match—washed jeans, a faded blue Valentino t-shirt and expensive crocodile shoes with no socks. It looked like the sun had not visited him for years, if ever. One could cut the tension with a knife, and clearly the idea of putting a game of Mexican Train, while not a bad idea, was ill timed with the present tension between Leo and Philip. In addition to this, it soon became clear that everyone was avoiding mentioning Tony's murder, but this did little to put a stop to the tension in the air.

Laura, to get past whatever disagreement occurred on their way over, got the domino box out and, after dumping the chips on the gaming table, announced, "Now, let's try to have a pleasant game… Let's forget what's just happened to Tony for a bit, if you don't mind as I suspect that everyone is on edge. I know I've certainly been. Everyone, let's turn the chips face down and then choose a geeker". Everyone got busy turning the domino chips so that they were all face down. There was some discussion as to which geeker Kathy should have, as she had trouble making up her mind. Philip suggested pink and Leo went for blue, "As it's Kathy 's favorite color." Finally, after picking up the pink geeker, fingering it and then putting it down, Kathy sighed and chose the blue one as she said, "Leo always makes the best decisions".

Laura, in an attempt to divert everyone's attention, said, "I wonder where Karl and Rebecca are?" Just as she said that, the doorbell rang and it was the missing guests. Laura, knowing that her different guests were not close friends and wanting to continue to distract Leo and Philip, rushed into the introductions, saying as she gestured towards the new arrivals. "Everyone, these are my special friends Rebecca and Karl, and this pretty lady here is Kathy, and this is her brother Philip, and this here is Leo, Kathy's… special friend."

Everyone shook hands, but it was clear that Leo was annoyed at his introduction, while Kathy just smiled and said, "Howdy, y'all."

Laura gestured for everyone to sit down around the table with Leo and Philip grabbing the chairs on either side of Kathy. Laura had predetermined that everyone knew how to play the game, so it was just a matter of taking the number twelve double domino and placing it in the center of the table as Laura announced, "Now everyone each take eleven domino tiles and let's all have some fun."

As everyone was setting up his and her tiles, Laura asked what everyone wanted to drink. Rebecca and Karl asked for club soda, Leo wanted a beer, Phillip wanted a white wine and Kathy wasn't sure and finally told Laura that she'd have "Whatever you're having, Honey."

Willis and Laura quickly got everyone drinks with Willis having wine and Laura opting to have a Coke.

Once everyone was settled in and had their chips selected and set up, Kathy was the first to play and she seemed confused. She had a twelve tile but hesitated as to where to play it. Leo was trying not to be annoyed, but did a bad job of hiding it and finally said, "For God's sake, just play your chip, Kathy." Kathy wavered and finally drawled, "Well you know me… I'm kinda squirrely when it comes to this game. What should I do?"

Leo leaned over, checked out her chips, tapped one of her chips and said, "Start the train with that one. It's the only move you have." Rebecca and Karl looked at each other and unknowingly registered a "What have we gotten ourselves into" look.

Laura put the chip out to start the train and said, "Thank you, Sugar." She smiled sweetly and then declared, "Well, I hope this will keep y'all happy." The move seemed to please Laura in particular, as it turned out she would not have been able to make a move without that opening move. Also, she hoped that everyone would settle down to a nice relaxed game.

The game progressed with Karl and Rebecca along with Laura and Willis trying to stay upbeat and positive while Leo and Philip alternated between being unhappy to being downright nasty to each other. The game quickly dissolved into some rather rude infighting between the two men, and Laura finally announced, "Playing this game was certainly a bad idea, and maybe we should just forget about it." There were nods all around, even from Kathy.

And so, by mutual consent, they began to pack up the game. Laura tried to keep things light, but everyone seemed to be on edge. Clearly Tony's death was on everyone's mind but no one wanted to talk about it. Finally, just to make conversation, Kathy said excitedly "I thought you'd all like to know, Leo is permanently moving in with me." Philip slammed his fist down on the table so hard that the remaining chips flew all over the place.

"That's just fucking great! You know Mom, I've told you that you and Leo aren't really married. That boat captain had no legal right to marry you two. Everyone here at Sunningdale knows it. Sorry to say, but you'll be shacking up with this..." And he was clearly at a loss of words as to what to call Leo until he came up with "This piece of shit!"

Leo got out of his chair so fast that it tipped over and was about to take a swing at Philip when Willis stepped in front of him, held him off, and tried to get him to settle down by saying, "Now let's calm down. I know everyone is on edge about Tony being killed, but let's stay civil to one another."

With that Laura said coolly "This obviously was a bad idea. I think it best if we call it a day."

"Fine with me," said Leo. "You coming with me, Kathy?"

"Oh, ah just don't know. What should I do, Laura?"

"If you want, you can stay here tonight. Willis is using the guestroom but you're welcome to use the sofa bed."

"No, Kathy's coming with me and we're going back to her place... Our place. Philip, clearly you're not wanted, so why don't you move out of the guestroom and leave your mother alone."

"No fucking way. I don't trust you with my mom. Did you know she's afraid of you, Leo?"

"Why you……"

And the argument continued as the three of them walked out the front door with Philip muttering, "I'm going to kill that guy one of these days! One could still hear them arguing even when they were outside with the front door closed.

"Well, that was quite the show. Not a great idea, I'm afraid, Laura," commented Willis.

Laura just shook her head and said, "I'm really sorry about all this. Do you think Kathy's safe with that guy?"

"Damned if I know, as I don't really understand the full story, but offhand I wouldn't trust Leo as far as I could throw him. Philip actually pulled me aside and suggested that Leo might have killed Tony. Needless to say, this is not a very safe situation for Kathy to be in. Too bad she doesn't have a mind of her own."

"Agreed," was all Laura could come up with.

Meanwhile Karl and Rebecca had been quietly looking on and it was obvious that they were both very disturbed and uncomfortable by all that had happened. Karl, being used to dealing with difficult people, said, "I'm glad I'm not involved with that soap opera. Poor Kathy... What a situation she's in and on top of Tony being murdered. It's all very upsetting. Laura, would you mind terribly if we took our leave?"

"Of course not. Maybe another day under better circumstances." And she showed them to the door.

When they were gone, Laura collapsed in a chair and said, "I don't ever remember being so tired… so exhausted." Looking at Willis, she said, "Would you mind terribly if I lie down for a bit?"

"Of course not. You tried to be helpful, but sometimes things are beyond one's help. I think I'll go for a walk if that's OK with you. Why don't you take that nap?"

Willis waited until Laura had gotten settled in her room and he quietly left the house. He thought about going over to Tony's house just to see if he could learn anything, but realized that the police would certainly have secured the murder scene. It was times like this when he missed not being on the Force when one could get needed information from the inside track.

Oh, well, there are always tradeoffs in this life, he thought. And so he walked a bit and finally decided to go over to the Tower to see if there was anything going on there. As he was entering the building he heard someone call "Willis!" and he looked to the right. There was Crayton waving his hand furiously and continuing to yell "Over here!"

When Willis caught up with him, Crayton proceeded to say, "We haven't formally met, but I'm Crayton. I recognize you because I saw you leaving Laura's earlier and she's told me all about you. Great to run into you. I was just over here checking on the food list for my Valentine's Day party.

You are coming to it, aren't you?"

Willis hadn't been sure if he was invited, but Laura had indicated that she wanted him to escort her to the big event, and so Willis kind of assumed that he would be going.

Consequently, Willis said, "Laura has asked me to be her date for the night so yes, I'm planning to attend."

"Excellent," beamed Crayton. "The more the merrier. How's your little investigation coming along, Inspector?

"Offhand, I'd have to say it's full of surprises."

"All good, I hope."

"Mostly," replied Willis, wondering where Crayton was going with this conversation. "Tell me, Crayton, how did you end up here in Sunningdale?"

"Interesting question, Willis... I'm assuming you prefer Willis rather than Inspector Willis."

"That's for sure, although I certainly have been wearing that hat while I've been here in Sunningdale. What's your take on the numerous rumors of there being unnatural deaths around here?"

"Wow, you don't beat around the bush, do you?"

"Ok, let me explain a bit about myself. I'm here at the request of Laura, who was a very close friend of my mother's. Laura has been concerned that there have been some unusual deaths here in Sunningdale... Not deaths by natural causes. And so she asked me to investigate."

"Now that's interesting!" replied Crayton. "So, how's it going?"

"I'd say that there are lots of leads, but I haven't been able to fully zero in on a suspect so far."

"So, you feel there have been a number of deaths here and there's a killer amongst us?"

"Looks that way. Certainly in the case of Tony. Any thoughts of your own as to who might be a murderer here as well?" Willis asked.

"Hmmm, before I answer that question, let me ask one of my own. For starters, who do you think has been actually murdered other than Tony?"

"While I suspect a few others, we certainly know that Tony was killed. That to me is sufficient evidence that there's a killer here. The question is who is the murderer. I'd really like your thoughts on this, Crayton."

"Oh, okay, I was trying to avoid this discussion as I tend to think out of sight, out of mind, and I prefer to think all is well here in Sunningdale. In truth I tend to be a bit myopic and right now all I can think of is putting on a really fabulous party."

"A party like yours must be very expensive. How do you manage that?"

"I have my resources."

Willis smiled and raised an eyebrow, indicating for

Crayton to go on.

Crayton said, "I've been very fortunate. I was the only child of parents who were wonderfully well off. Consequently, I've always associated with very successful people, gone to the best schools, you know, traveled in a certain circle. When my parents died, they left me a considerable amount of money and since then, I've inherited even more from a special friend."

Crayton looked off to the side as if remembering someone unique, and finally went on to say, "I find myself here in Sunningdale with no family, no ties or responsibilities, and lots of financial resources, so why not have some fun with it?" He said that with a sort of edgy laugh as if he were talking to someone who could never understand him and, in truth, Willis really could not fully relate to such a situation.

Willis smiled and proceeded to ask, "How many people have you invited?

"Oh, I'd say maybe 150 or so. No, maybe 175."

"All residents of Sunningdale?"

"Oh gosh, no. There are a number of folks from the nearby Yacht Club. Hmmm, maybe a few dozen. You know, folks I know there, as I'm a member." He said rather conceitedly.

"Anyone else?"

"Oh, a few friends from out of town. You see, last year's party was such a hit, that word got around that it was THE party of the year and what could I do? I had a lot a pressure put on me to expand the festivities. Last year we had a dance floor with recorded music but this year I've added a live band." He said this rather smugly, and then rather grandly stated, "This will be THE party. NOTHING can stop it from being the best event of the year!"

Willis asked, "So is everyone invited?"

Crayton replied, "Well... no. I want people like Else and, of couse, Laura. But in answer to your question, no. Let's face it, not everyone is a good fit for us. I don't mean to be an elitist, but some folks here really don't really fit in."

"Like who, for example?"

"Well, let me think... Ah, do you know a guy here named Bruton? He's the guy who feeds the birds all the time... Very anti-social... Not someone who would be a plus factor at my party. You know that water bottle he always carries with him?"

Willis nodded his head.

"Well, he says he had an operation for cancer of his mouth and that they destroyed the glands that produce saliva. Consequently, he needs to lubricate his mouth with water all the time. Well, according to Alice, who works in the infirmary, that's bullshit. He never had such a condition or operation. That bottle he carries with him is nothing more than vodka, and between you and me, it certainly affects his behavior. He can be really nasty and evil when he has too much of his 'water.'" Crayton raised his hands and made quotation marks with his fingers.

"And so, no, I have not invited him. Of course, it's not like I have guards at the doors, but he knows that he's not invited, not wanted. I only want fun, really nice, smart people at my fête, and I've all but told him so."

Other than that piece of gossip, it was clear that Crayton would be of little use to Willis and his investigation. Little did Crayton—nor Willis, for that matter—know how memorable the party would be and not for the right reasons.

Tuesday—Day Seven
The Heart of the Matter

The day started in much same manner as the other days for Willis. He got up early, grabbed a cup of coffee, and went back to his room, showered and shaved and dressed for the day. His plan was to do some additional research and later change and dress for the party.

When he offered to help Laura, it turned out that there wasn't much for Willis to do, as Crayton and Laura had everything well in hand. Consequently, Willis spent most of the day working on his computer, researching some medical case studies that he found so fascinating that he had a hard time pulling away from it to go to the party.

Earlier Laura had explained to Willis that Crayton had asked her to be the Chairperson of the Valentine 's Day Party. The idea was to raise money for the staff, as tipping was not allowed. The event was to occur today, Saint Valentine's Day. Again, as in past years, everyone was requested to wear either red, white, or black or any combination of the three.

It turned out that the Sunningdale staff, who had been assigned to help with the party, had outdone themselves. At Laura's request, the staff had set up a black and white checked dance floor, food stations, and high-top tables draped in a red stretch fabric. On each table there was a tall white orchid plant, which made it possible for those unable to stand for any length of time to sit on the tall stools and see what was going on around them without having to deal with craning their necks to see around the flowers.

At one point Laura asked Willis for his opinion. She said, "You know Bruton, the man who feeds the birds all the time, well he's clearly a bit of a misfit in Sunningdale and quite anti-social so I stupidly discouraged Crayton from inviting him. Now I'm having second thoughts about ostracizing him from the festivities, but it's clearly too late to extend an invitation to him. What would you do, Willis?"

Willis thought, *While Laura is concerned that she might*

have caused Bruton to be upset, there are so many people involved, there's bound to be someone whose feelings will be hurt because of not being invited. And so he said, "I wouldn't worry too much about him, as he's such a misfit, he surely won't want to be part of the party. Crayton, on the other hand, fascinates me in that he seems so caught up in this party and impressing people."

Laura smiled and said, "Yes, it would seem that way, but there's a totally other side to him that most people aren't aware of."

"Oh" said Willis "Like what?"

"Hmmm, let me see. There are two stories that come to mind. Crayton is very secretive about the good things he does, but I hear about them from my hairdresser, you know the man who chopped off half my hair when he reached for the wrong scissors. Anyway, he and Crayton are very close friends and he's told me some interesting things that Crayton keeps under wraps."

"Oh? Willis asked.

"Well, Crayton has a friend who is very sick. The guy is in the hospital and probably won't ever get out. It's just a matter of time. The poor guy is broke and just hanging on. Well, Crayton, when he heard this, went to his bank, took out some money, $10,000.00 to be exact, and wrapped it up in some gift paper he had and gave it to the guy. Apparently, Crayton at the end of visiting the guy, just handed him the package and said, 'Hey, I had this lying around the house and I don't have any need for it, so I thought you could use it.' And gave him a hug and left before the guy could open the package."

"Another time, Crayton had a friend who had a degenerative disease where he was having great difficulty walking. The poor guy was crazed with anxiety. He had gone to Goodwill and bought a really beat-up wheelchair which was falling apart. One day, Crayton called him and asked him if he'd like to go for a ride. The guy who hardly got around was very pleased. Well, Crayton took him to a place that specialized in merchandise for people with a disability and he bought the guy the best wheelchair in the place... One with all the bells and whistles and wouldn't take 'no' for an answer from the guy. The only criteria was the guy had to swear that he would never tell anyone how he got it. Pretty wonderful I'd say, but you know how word gets around. Oh, and I just heard that he is working on a way to help Hal with his finances if he eventually is able to get that heart transplant... Wonderful!"

Willis said, "Well, that certainly gives me some interesting insight into Crayton. Thanks."

Later, back in his room, Willis was deep into reading more about DID, when he heard a shriek that could only have come from Laura. He raced through the villa and finally found her out in the yard, hysterical. She had gone to water her beloved bonsai before getting dressed for the party and was standing there looking at the plant, or what was left of it. It had been violently ripped apart; the pot smashed to pieces.

Willis instinctively reached over to comfort her and asked in a deeply concerned voice, "What happened?"

Laura said, "I… I don't know. My wonderful bonsai has been destroyed. Why? Why would anyone do such a terrible thing? Why am I being punished? Am I going crazy? Oh, Willis, help me!"

He took her in his arms and tried to calm her down and at the same time tried to figure out what was going on when he noticed that her hands were cut and bruised. *Was that from trying to save the plant?* Willis thought. A second thought entered his mind even though he didn't want to think it. *Could she have destroyed the plant herself?*

He led her to her room and got her to lie down. He went to the kitchen, got a hand towel, soaked it in warm water and brought it to her so she could try to clean up her hands. After that, he put a comforter over her and suggested that she try to rest a bit despite the fact that the party was due to begin in four hours or so. He then said, "I'll call you in an hour's time so you can get ready for the party."

Thank God, he thought, *her work is done. No need for her to be there early.*

Willis spent the next hour or so wracking his brain for an answer as to what was going on. In truth, he had a strong suspicion, but was hoping that he was wrong. He eventually went to knock on her bedroom door, but there was no answer, so Willis went to his room scratching his head. He got dressed and when he came out, he spotted a note taped on a chair that had been moved just inside the front door so there was no chance he could miss it. The note simply said:

Willis,
I've gone over to the party to check to make sure everything has been set up properly.
See you there.
I love you and hope that you'll never forget that.
Laura

Willis found the note to be both assuring and disturbing. He tucked It into his pocket, took the elevator to the third floor, and walked down the hallway to the party room. As he entered the room he stopped dead in his tracks....The place looked spectacular… truly amazing! The ceiling was a mass of red and white heart-shaped balloons, many with red, white, and black ribbons trailing downwards as if trying to join the sea of guests in their party attire that echoed the color theme.

The place was already packed! He soon spotted Hal, who clearly was having trouble walking but had joined the party and had on a black tuxedo with a red bow tie and cummerbund, red socks, and even a red cane! He was talking with Laura who was in a chic, bright red dress that reeked of class. It had a collar which she had turned up so it framed her beautiful face. The dress accentuated her small waist and there were panels that descended to the ground from the waist band which alternated, some covered with small jewels, and some were just plane fabric. All very stylish and chic.

The outfit clearly had cost a great deal of money, and while Willis was never of the mind to spend much on his own clothes, in this case he fully approved of every penny she must have spent on hers. She looked sensational, and he went over to tell her just that. As he approached her, he noted that she had on her special perfume which perfectly enhanced her persona. She projected a calm, incredibly polished woman totally in charge. One would never know that she had been so upset earlier? *Remarkable…Who is this woman and can I have a future with her?* Willis mused.

The music, provided by a small band of musicians all dressed in white, was perfect as it was not excessively loud and yet it gave an energy to the party. It also had a hint of an echo to its sound which made it sound inadvertently eerie. Laura had arranged for the Sunningdale kitchen to make an attractive assortment of hors d'oeuvres that were passed around by the staff who had joined in the fun by wearing their own red, white or black outfits.

There was also a large table loaded with an assortment of cheeses, crackers, breads, fresh shrimp, plus a selection of fruits and nuts and numerous trays of exotic and appetizing food, including a wide selection of mini heart-shaped sandwiches. At one end of the room was a bar which had two handsome bartenders from the Sunningdale staff. Both men were in red, black and white.

They had cut their shirts and pants down the middle vertically and had one of their girlfriends sew the clothes together so that one man was wearing half a red shirt and pants sewn to half a white shirt and pants. The other man had his half in black sewn to half a white shirt and pants. To finish it off, each man had painted half his face to go along with his outfit... Fun and it represented the support the Sunningdale help had brought to the event.

As for the guests, Else had a cocktail length white dress with a full skirt that had slits in it so that when she moved, panels of red and sometimes black would appear and then disappear. Very glamorous and unique. As one looked over the room, one saw a sea of red, black and white... No other colors… Overall, the crowd was clearly caught up in the excitement and fun of it all!

Earlier, when Willis had first heard about the party and the fun dress code, he had gone out and bought a bright red shirt and a pair of white pants to go with his black sports jacket. Earlier in the day, Laura, seeing his outfit on a hanger attached to the knob of the guest closet, gestured for Willis to "Wait right there" and she soon returned and produced a red handkerchief and proceeded to arrange it in the pocket of his black sports jacket. Both beamed with pleasure and enjoyed a sense of excitement about sharing the coming event together.

It was clearly a high-energy happening and everyone seemed set to have an unusually good time! Many of Sunningdale's members had seldom been to a theme party like this except for the lucky ones who had attended the previous year's Valentine's bash which had been a huge success. This year's party had grown from 75 guests to what now looked to be over 200. The party was clearly going to be the event of the year!

As the crowd grew in size, the sound grew accordingly. Everyone was having a terrific time. Soon Willis was deep in conversation with Felicia and Matty. Felicia was dazzling in a red satin man's tuxedo and extremely high heeled black shoes and a white fluffy lace cravat. Matty, on the other hand, was in an ill-fitting red blouse and black pants, which did nothing to hide her overweight figure. They posed strangely contrasting figures as Felicia was the epitome of femininity while Matty projected a somewhat masculine image which, needless to say, was less than flattering.

Interesting how Matty can be so smart and yet devoid of any sense of taste and style, thought Willis. While they were discussing past events, he discovered that Felicia had been out of town when Tony had been murdered, so it appeared that she was not a likely suspect.

Suddenly, Willis instinctively realized that he hadn't seen Laura for quite a while and, while looking around the room he saw a woman dressed in a very large flowing gown that was totally black, including a hat that covered her hair. The woman also strangely wore a pair of dark-tinted sunglasses with lenses that were heart-shaped, similar to the ones Lolita wore in the movie by the same name.

She also wore a mask that looked like a silver skull... eerie, bizarre, and unnerving. What the hell was the woman thinking? The overall effect was mysterious and quite in contrast to the rest of the guests.

Willis was drawn to the lady, but by then the place was very crowded and he had difficulty getting close to her. However, for a brief moment, he got near enough to her to smell her perfume, which was exactly the special one typically favored by and only worn by Laura. It was then that Willis—to his horror—knew in his gut that something horrendous was happening and he was devastated! It was Laura!

He tried to work his way closer to her, but now could no longer get near to her as she worked her way through the crowds. As she did, he could see that she was systematically reaching into the black basket on her arm and handing out large, red heart-shaped cookies to certain people. At one point she spotted Matty and offered her a cookie. Matty took the cookie but, being the astute lady she was, caught a whiff of the perfume she was wearing and, knowing that it was the perfume that was only worn by Laura, held the cookie and said, "Thanks, Laura, but on second thought, no thanks. By the way, that skull mask and heart-shaped sunglasses make you look really bizarre."

With that she spun around, leaving Matty with her un-eaten cookie and offered another cookie to Felicia. Willis tried to get closer but the crowd closed in between them. In desperation, Willis shouted at the top of his lungs...

"LAURA, STOP!"

She whirled around and tried to work her way through the crowd to flee. When she couldn't escape, she suddenly took two of the cookies out of her basket, lifted her mask just enough and desperately ate them as fast as she could. She continued to try to escape but the crowd was too thick.

Suddenly, she staggered and collapsed on the floor in a pile of black writhing fabric that came apart to reveal her red outfit underneath. Willis quickly shouted, "BACK OFF, BACK OFF EVERYONE SO LAURA CAN BREATHE!" but it was too late.

As she twisted and writhed wildly, she appeared to be close to death! Willis gently but with considerable difficulty, removed the mask, the glasses, and the hat, and it was clear that the person was none other than Bruton! As Willis cradled his head, Bruton tried to say something, but his voice was very weak.

But by leaning close to him, Willis finally heard him say, "I just... I just had to kill them. They were all so evil... so bad!... They were so.... mean." And with that he died! Clearly the heart-shaped cookies were poison.

Willis screamed at the top of his voice, "IF ANYONE RECEIVED A HEART-SHAPED COOKIE, YOU MUST NOT EAT IT! THE COOKIES ARE POISONED AND THEY WILL KILL YOU! THE POLICE WILL NEED THEM FOR EVIDENCE. PLEASE GIVE THE COOKIES OVER TO ME."

Matty stood nearby, clutching her heart-shaped cookie. She gripped it so tightly that it quickly began to crumble. Willis desperately asked if anyone could get him a bag, and as soon as he had one, he quickly started collecting as many heart-shaped cookies as he could as evidence for the police.

There was a great deal of confusion with people being very upset. Many shouted, "DON'T EAT THE HEART-SHAPED COOKIES!" Pandemonium quickly spread. Some people fled, while others stood around transfixed by what they were seeing. It turned out that Felicia had eaten just a small bite of one of the cookies, but it was only for show as she was on one of her constantly reoccurring diets and had just made the gesture to be polite.

After she took the bite, she planned to take the remainder of the cookie, wrap it in a cocktail napkin, and discard it on one of the top hat tables. However, she had eaten enough to get violently ill and had to be rushed to the nearby Sarasota Memorial Hospital. where she eventually recovered.

Hal wasn't so fortunate, as he had eaten a whole cookie and collapsed, writhing in pain before quickly dying. The police, of course, were called, and soon the sounds of numerous police sirens were added to the drama and the confusion. Names and addresses were taken and the party quickly broke up with the exception of a number of hangers-on who stood around and couldn't get enough of the drama of it all.

Willis spent a considerable time late that evening explaining to the police what had happened and why. It had been a long and exhausting evening, and he couldn't wait to call it a day. All during this time, he was frantic to find Laura, as she was not answering his many phone calls.

It turned out that she had left her phone at home, and during the turmoil had remained at the party, comforting several of the guests. Eventually, she worked her way back to the villa where she retrieved her phone. She immediately called Willis and asked that he get back to her place "As soon as possible."

Willis finally was able to break away from the meeting with the police and returned to the villa. He found her sitting quietly in her office, writing in her journal. When she heard him arrive, she threw the journal on the floor and rushed into his arms. They remained that way for a long time, trying to draw strength from each other. Later, they sat quietly as each filled in the other one with what they saw and what they knew… each trying to make sense of the strangeness of the night. It all remained a mystery until details emerged over the next twenty-four hours or so.

Wednesday—Day Eight
Rest in Peace

The next day proved to be a very sober one, as everyone was in a daze. It was like a gray cloud had descended over Sunningdale. Most everyone appeared to be inclined to keep his or her thoughts private, which certainly was not typical of the inhabitants, but there were, of course, lots of rumors and cell calls. As a result, Willis called a gathering to take place in one of the community center's meeting rooms late that Wednesday afternoon, using a list of the persons who had been invited to the party.

To Willis's amazement, almost everyone showed up, plus some who had not been at the party but were dying to hear the details. It appeared that there was little interaction among the attendees. For a change, they were a sober and not a very gregarious lot.

After everyone was seated, Willis got up on stage and, holding a microphone as well as a paper with the following statement, he addressed the group:

"I want to thank you all for joining us this afternoon on what has to be a rather strange and disturbing time for everyone. For those who don't know me, my name is Willis. Some call me Inspector Willis but I mostly prefer Willis. In my former life I was a police inspector but have since left the force and started my own company called "The 3 in 1 Investigating Company." I was brought here at the request of Laura Wilk."

As he said this, he made a gesture towards her sitting in the third row and found himself smiling despite the seriousness of the meeting. "Laura had been a great friend of my mother's before my mother passed away. She brought me here because she was disturbed about a group of questionable deaths that were taking place here in Sunningdale."

A few people in the audience nodded and even exchanged a few whispered comments, but most remained quiet and very attentive.

Willis went on to say, "At first, I was suspicious as to just to how valid were Laura's concerns. After all, In an Assisted Living Facility, one expects a certain number of its older residents to pass away. But upon examining some of the deaths, a certain pattern seemed to emerge that supported Laura's concern. At first, I suspected a number of Laura's friends."

Willis looked at Matty, Else, and Felicia, who were sitting in the first few rows and said, "Sorry, folks, but in various ways you all looked suspicious, but in the long run no one fit the bill. Meanwhile, Laura seemed to get increasingly disturbed about the deaths. When Claudine was killed by eating a poisoned peach and then Tony was strangled with the white piece of cloth, I became convinced that Laura's fears were certainly valid and well-founded. There clearly was a murderer in our midst but who? We now know that it was Bruton."

"I want to apologize to everyone for taking so long to stop the murderer. This was just one of those really difficult cases, and I'm sorry that all of you were exposed to his potential threat. Suffice it to say that the police and I are 100% certain that Bruton was the killer and that he acted on his own. In short, you are now all safe."

There was an enthusiastic round of applause.

"When I leave here, I will be going down to the police headquarters to make a final statement. I cannot say how grateful I am that no one else will get hurt, and again I assure you that you're all safe."

There was another round of applause and finally, when Willis was able to quiet them down, with a bit of a wicked smile on his face, he looked over at Crayton and said, "I wonder what Crayton here will dream up next year to top this year's Valentine's Day party!"

The audience roared with laughter as Willis gave a wave and left the stage.

He walked over to Laura, gave her a big hug and a kiss on the cheek and said, "I won't be long. How about a small celebratory dinner over at Saint Armand's Circle this evening when I get back?" to which Laura nodded, agreeing enthusiastically.

Willis made his way down to the police station and was escorted to a small meeting room where a collection of officers was gathered. He was introduced to everyone by Inspector Harris. Willis did his best to fill in the details of the case.

When he was finished, Harris took over and said, "Willis here has been remarkably helpful. For example, when we first entered this case that involved Rosaline O' Connor and her supposed accident where she rushed from the kitchen where she was cutting up an orange and tripped while carrying the knife and accidentally mortally stabbed herself, Willis here asked if the knife had any residual orange on it. We checked the records and, by God, it didn't!"

"It was then we started to look more carefully into the deaths that were occurring in Sunningdale. Last night several of us went over to Bruton Manchester's home and secured it. Early this morning we pretty much tore the place apart. Among the interesting things we discovered were a considerable number of 'water bottles' filled with vodka. It turns out that Bruton clearly had a serious drinking problem."

"We also found a selection of books on poisons along with a bulletin board hanging on the wall that had various daily reminders posted on it. When we flipped the board over, there was a collection of 3 by 5 cards each with the name of a person on it. Included were:

Herb Talmon
Helen Cronin
Rosaline O'Connor
Claudine Hollar
Tony Stewart

"Each of these cards had a huge red "X" across it… all people who had been killed.

Among the other cards on the board were:

Hal Snyder—who unfortunately died from one of the poisoned cookies

Felicia Ross—who is currently in the hospital but is expected to recover

Laura Wilk

Matty King

Else Carning

Crayton Williams III

And...

Inspector Willis

"Luckily, Bruton didn't get to kill any more folks in Sunningdale. Or did he? We'll never know if there were, in fact, other victims, and that thought haunts us all. Well, as difficult as this case has been, it's over. Willis here stopped the killer despite a somewhat misleading series of events."

Willis smiled at this, as he still wasn't a hundred percent sure that the force was behind him, as he had initially held back on revealing the evidence of the poison on the peaches, not to mention his misplaced suspicion regarding the woman at home who has a mild case of DID. Life is for sure a complicated journey.

"Willis, we here at the force thank you for your help in this very odd and difficult case. In many ways we feel you are part of our force."

There was some polite applause led by Harris, and there were smiles and handshakes all around. There were a few more inquiries, mostly generated out of curiosity, and soon Willis was free to leave. He drove slowly back to Laura's place deep in thought and filled with a gratefulness that was slowly enveloping him. He realized that not only were the crimes resolved, but a whole new chapter to his life appeared to be about to open up.

As Willis drove up, he saw Laura in the garden watering a new bonsai plant.

"I see the plant I ordered has arrived," he said with a grin which was topped by the shy smile on Laura's face.

"Well, aren't you the sneaky one, Inspector!" she said. "So how did it go down at the Station?"

Willis resisted commenting about how expensive the bonsai had been. At this point, he wanted the world for her, no matter the cost.

"Ok, I guess. Of course, I would have liked it if I had really nailed the criminal."

"Oh, so you mean that you wish it had been me who was the killer?"

"You know I didn't mean that!"

"Well, it sure sounded like that."

"Oh, come on, Laura you know what I mean."

"I'm not so sure, Willis." She stood up and headed for the door.

"Please stay with me on this." There was a long pause and finally Willis in desperation said, "Do you really want to know what I thought as this whole thing evolved?" as he gestured for her to take a seat.

"You better believe it." She said crossing her arms across her chest as she impatiently sat down.

He took a deep breath and said, "OK, here goes, but you probably won't like what I say. You might even change your mind about us when I confess to you what I was really thinking."

He took another deep breath and said with a grimace. "To be perfectly honest, at one point I was pretty convinced that you suffered from DID or Dissociative Identity Disorder and that you probably were the murderer."

This did not appear to sit well with her and she adjusted her seat, smoothed her skirt, and said, "OK, Mister Inspector… explain yourself."

Willis took her hand and said, "DID or Dissociative Identity Disorder is a very rare condition where a person has a number of different individual personalities. The reason that I first started to think you might be a candidate for this is the fact that your husband used to come home from his business trips and say, 'I wonder what person Laura will be this time, as she seems to have several personalities.'"

Laura continued to sit there with her arms crossed and said, "Go on, Willis."

Willis started to sweat. "Well, when I saw the person in gray clothes painting the fruit on Claudine Hollar's tree and I later saw similar gray clothes in your guest room... Well, you never wear gray clothing... clothes that lack color. Then, of course, you removed them from my room and so I started to develop some more suspicions. When Tony was strangled—reportedly by a white piece of cloth—it was around that time that you stopped wearing your white bathrobe that had a white cloth belt."

"I surreptitiously tried to check your bathrobe to see if the belt was missing, sorry about that, but you told me that the robe had been sent to the cleaners as there was a spot on it that you couldn't remove. A suspicious explanation I'd say, but a lead I couldn't easily follow up on. So much for that. You have to understand Laura..." And Willis started to tear up, "I was beside myself. I was falling deeper and deeper in love with you and I was also getting more and more convinced that you were the killer. I didn't know what to do!"

"Ah, the famous inspector Willis… confused. Hmmm,"

said Laura with a hint of mischievous sarcasm. Then, realizing how upset he was becoming, she gently squeezed his arm and said, "Go on, Willis."

"When you told me how you were molested as a young child and then not wanting children of your own, which by the way is typical of women who have been molested... this is a pattern that is often found in people with DID, Dissociative Identity Disorder."

Willis continued, but the more he tried to explain his concerns, the more upset he got, as he wanted desperately to explain how someone in his position works and thinks, but everything he said and did was colored by his growing love for this marvelous woman and his eyes began to tear up at the thought of hurting her or maybe even losing her love.

When Laura realized this, she reached over and took Willis's hand and gave it a squeeze. "Oh, you're such a dear, sweet, loving man. The truth is, my husband and I wanted children but I couldn't somehow conceive." She said this with a rather sad shrug.

"Not to worry, my love for you echoes yours. In any case, I somehow have the feeling that your partners Ross and Monty might, if we're lucky, adopt us as parents. Stranger things have happened," she said with a mischievous smile. "As for DID, Dissociative Identity Disorder, you're partially right in that I have a slight case of DID. That is, I have two personalities within me who are both similar and yet dissimilar. Luckily, I'm totally aware of this condition and both of us want you in our lives."

Willis developed a slight smile on his face and was tempted to ask which personality he had gone to bed with the other night, but opted to postpone that question for a more opportune time. However, he couldn't help wondering if her having two personalities meant that their sex life would have more than the normal amount of variations… a delicious thought!

Meanwhile, he was unaware of the huge sigh of relief that he let out as he processed what he had just heard. He knew he had just turned a page in his life. Here he was with this wonderful, unique woman who was smart, charming, beautiful and very, VERY special. Maybe he just connected with two such people… two in one but who knows… who cares. Each one he had seen to date was remarkable, special, and most important, lovable. Clearly, he was about to start a new chapter his life and its title was:

"Laura"

He looked at her, smiled, and took her hand even though he wasn't sure which Laura he was holding. Regardless, he couldn't wait to find out as he turned the next page.

About the Author

Ray Klausen has had a wide and varied background ranging from being a top television and theater set designer for over 400 productions, including nine Broadway shows and 10 Academy Award productions, resulting in his winning three Emmy Awards. He has worked with such celebrities as: Michael Jackson, Prince, Cher, Bea Arthur, Barbara Streisand, Madonna, and Elvis, to name a few.

His first book, *Behind the Scenes: From Hollywood to Broadway*, is a remarkable history of the television theater world from the late 1970s to the early 21st Century. Previous novels include: *Duplicity, Duplicity in 3 Acts,* and *Deep Duplicity.* All are "An Inspector Willis Murder Mystery".

A note from the author:

When I began *Duplicity, Care to Die*, I had come across an article about DID or Dissociative Identity Disorder which fascinated me. It's a very rare condition where a person can develop a second, and in some cases, many additional personalities. The person who has this condition can have personalities that vary even in terms of sex, interests, and so forth. I asked myself what would happen if the person's personalities were such that one was exceptionally good and kind and the alternate personality evil and bad? What if the person's personalities were in conflict with each other?

While I don't pretend to understand the full ramifications of DID in a situation such as this, I felt it made for a fascinating conundrum, a circumstance worth exploring. Could my character Laura be suffering from DID? Ultimately, when discussing this with a very knowledgeable doctor, I found out that not only was DID very rare, but it's almost unheard of for a person with that condition to ever be violent or murderous. So much for going that route!

What I did find out was that murderers can often have a drinking problem and can be antisocial. And so, I had my killer. Also, along the way I found myself more than a bit enamored with Laura and I'm hoping that she and Willis make it into *Double Duplicity*, the next book in this series. We'll see... it's a mystery.

—Ray Klausen

Coming soon:

Inspector Willis's next adventure

Double Duplicity

Also by Ray Klausen

Published by Amarna Books and Media